I0625982

REVENGE
of the
LUSHITES

Russ Crossley

53RD STREET PUBLISHING

Revenge of the Lushites

Russ Crossley

Copyright 2013 Russ Crossley

All rights reserved
Cover art: © Charles Nemitz
Cover Design by R. Edgewood
Cover and interior layout
Copyright © 2014 by 53rd Street Publishing

Trade paperback ISBN 978-1-927621-26-4

Ebook ISBN 9781458197191

This is a work of fiction. The persons and situations are products of the author's imagination,

Published by 53rd Street Publishing
www.53rdstreetpublising.com
Logo image by:

Engraver | Dreamstime.com

Introduction

This story had its genesis at a workshop taught by my mentors Dean Wesley Smith and Kristine Katherine Rusch too many years ago to talk about. I had written a short story based on the idea of the fast food companies running the galaxy. The story, *Big Business*, can be found on most on-line bookstore sites. I then wrote a novel proposal for *Attack of the Lushites*.

My initial goal was to use a science fiction setting to talk about addiction an issue close to my heart because I have been addicted to a few things in my own life (no, not drugs) so I was familiar with the thought process of an addict. I didn't want to be preachy about the dangers of drugs (prescription and non-prescription) or alcohol or tobacco or anything else as this has been done my many people far more qualified than I.

I thought I'd use satire as a vehicle to tell a story and set my story in the far future. Both Dean and Kris encouraged me to go over the top when I wrote the first novel proposal. I did this and discovered not only an audience, but some wonderful characters who I really enjoyed writing about.

Unfortunately (or fortunately depending on how you look at such things) New York publishers loved the work but were hesitant to publish humorous science fiction because they don't feel fans of the genre will buy humor. (Anyone ever heard of *Galaxy Quest,* or The *Big Bang Theory,* or *The Hitchhikers Guide to the Galaxy*?)

With recent changes to publishing *Attack of the Lushites* is available in trade paperback and ebook with a fantastic cover by Charles Nemitz.

After I finished the first novel I knew I had to write sequels. What you hold in your hands (or see on your e-reader) is the first sequel set more than one thousand years after the first novel ended. My intention is to set each novel a thousand years in the future from the last one. Where will it end? I have no idea.

One note that my very wonderful editor cautioned me about is my occasional use of reader notes (for the ebook versions) and footnotes for the print version to explain some oddity in these future societies. I make no apology for them because I think they're necessary and funny so if you don't like them please feel free to write your own book then you can do want you want.

So enough of the background let's get the story started. Enjoy the ride and regardless if you like this story or don't feel to contact me on Facebook, twitter or via my publishers website.

Russ Crossley
Vancouver Canada
2013

Cast of Principal Characters

Piper Cleaner — First Assistant to the Assistant Surveillance Officer, a Methanite from the planet Methane, who lives to work less and smoke more. Unfortunately for him he is the reluctant hero called to adventure in this story. He is far from the hero type but what's a guy to do?

Smokey Cigarillo — A human from the planet Dirt in the Sol system. She is a schemer and dreamer who dreams of power and will do anything it takes to achieve her ambitions, but at what price?

Admiral Awesome — Human, also from Dirt, ambitious with a poor work ethic, and he's a coward under fire. Promoted because no one else wanted the job he's the Decorated Admiral of the Grand Fleet of the Tobacco Galaxy.

Cherry Bomb — A female very long lived, four-armed, crimson-skinned alien from an unidentified destroyed planet. A former security specialist (she has a muscular build) she became a propulsion scientist and has developed a new ship design that could change intergalactic travel. But will she share the new technology or use it for personal gain?

Trixie Pug — Human from Dirt now resides on Snackcake III in the Lushite galaxy. Former President of Heavenly Sky Burger she's been lost in the Garbage galaxy for a thousand years (local time). Claims to no longer have ambitions for the absolute power she sought a millennium ago but is she telling the truth?

Herman Pug — Human originally from Dirt. Brilliant propulsion scientist who invented the Flash-o-Matic 3000 intergalactic ship. Now resides on planet Four in the Mega Jumbo Pack System. Has been in suspended animation for a thousand years. Will he help Piper avert disaster or does he have his own plans?

Cyber Drive — Alien captain of the *L.S.S. Whiskey Bottle*. A virtual gamer who would rather fight virtual battles than real ones. He befriends Piper when they meet and becomes an ally, but is he going to be helpful in the real world?

The Brain — Artificial Intelligence who can assume any shape or size using a holo-projection. Every race in two galaxies has Brain's to seek advice from and to help with daily tasks. But do they have their own plans for the galaxy?

Prologue

"It's like stealing smokes from a baby. Easy peasey."
– Emperor Bud Wiser the First describing how he conquered a newly discovered planet.

March, 4444 and 1/4

PIPER CLEANER LEANED BACK in the form-fitted secure-a-chair provided for him by Galaxy Tobacco, closed his brown eyes, and eased into the loving grip of the pillowy soft chair cushions. His long fingers gripped the burning cigarette hanging from one side of his pursed, yellow lips. He blew a ring of acrid smoke, directing it at the ceiling of the comm center, then took the smoldering tobacco stick from his lips and placed it on the ashtray recessed into the console.

Piper's taut skin was the color of a pale banana, his hair was the shade of grape juice, and he had the six-toed feature on his left foot so common to Methanites. This meant the silver space boots he was issued when he arrived at this outpost had to be modified to fit him. His left boot was slightly larger than his left and it took him time to get used to shuffling his lanky form around the plasti-steel decks in the .86 gravity of the six level station.

Piper was tall for his race, nearly six-foot five, but he was also very thin for his race, in one gravity he only weighted a hundred fifty pounds.

He'd been assigned as the assistant to the assistant surveillance officer for the past two years on the Smoky Eye Surveillance Outpost at the edge of the galaxy. Compared with Piper's home planet, Methane, the luxurious surveillance post was incredibly comfortable and much less smelly.

The outpost's purpose was to detect any incoming threats to the galaxy originating from deep space. It had been more than a thousand years since the Lushites invaded the galaxy and changed everything, but there had been rumors they might return at any time.

"Life is good," Piper sighed to himself as he took another drag on his cigarette.

His whisper echoed off the wall-sized screens surrounding the chair where he sat in the middle of the donut shaped control room.

This outpost, serial number 3.103.243.9, was one of three thousand such outposts guarding the galactic rim. Everything in the outpost was labeled (just like the auto-credits transferred to Piper's account every month) PROPERTY OF GALAXY TOBACCO with a line of fine print running along the edge of the bottom of the label: KEEP YOUR NICOTINE-STAINED DIGITS TO YOURSELF.

If you traced the money (Rule Number One: always follow the money), you'd discover that the Tobacco Sellers and Distributors funded the outposts for A Better Universe, an industry lobbyist group.

Not that Piper cared. He loved this job. There was never any real work to do, so he could smoke all day and get paid. Best of all they provided all the smokes you could use for free! Yes, siree this was the dream job of dream jobs.

"Huh, sir..."

One purple eyebrow rose up Piper's light, banana-yellow forehead. He hated it when the outpost's central computer bothered him.[1]

The Brain loved watching the comets and asteroids that sometimes passed through the outposts' six parsecs of survey area. Once he even spotted a rogue planet. But who cared about such crap? Not Piper. He had bigger stogies to smoke. Like on his next smoke break.

He stole a glance at the time display on the wall over the bank of monitors. Ten minutes and counting. He licked his lips.

You couldn't smoke a comet or an asteroid, and the rogue planet was lifeless with no evidence of tobacco cultivation. Brain said the planet was an artificially created ball of reeking toxic garbage that had been circling the galaxy for over a thousand years. But the records were lost, and no one knew who created it.

Why should I care about useless information? "Hey, Brain, what's up?" Piper smirked.

"Well, I think you may wish to see this?"

The Brain's attitude really annoyed Piper no end. Sure The Brains had been installed in every marketeer ship, outpost, space station, and smoking parlor in the galaxy, and they were smart, but they were also mister know-it-alls. They were really annoying.

Piper sighed and leaned forward in his chair to stare at the screen directly in front of him. The monitor displayed nothing but untwinkling stars and ink-black space. As usual in the distance was the bright star that was Planet Five in the Pink Leaves System, the nearest system to this outpost. The outpost itself was built on an airless rogue moon roaming far outside any star system.

---

1   *Note to reader: every artificial intelligence is by tradition named, The Brain. The reasoning for the tradition is lost in the mists of time, but historians suggest it started sometime in the 27th century.*

The barren rocky moon was held in place by the gravitational forces of three nearby red giant stars. There were occasional tremors but nothing to worry about.

"Brain. I really don't have time for games right now. I'm busy."

As he spoke, Piper lit another cigarette with the one he was just finishing and stubbed the old one out in the ashtray built into the arm of the chair. The odor of ash wafted up his nose until the ashtray swallowed the butt and the ash and snapped shut. The residue would be sucked into the outposts disposal system, reduced to its atomic components, then flushed into space.

"OK, sir, but check out the screen behind you."

Piper covered his mouth with his fist, coughed then swung his chair around to face the screen Brain wanted him to look at, and froze. The image the computer had extrapolated from the sensor data stream coming into the outpost via the network of sensor satellites covering a billion square miles of space was completely unbelievable.

His mouth dropped open and the freshly lit cigarette dangling from his lip fell to the deck where the emergency fire suppression system immediately put it out.

The cigarette forgotten, Piper licked his suddenly dry lips. "Huh, Brain, is that what I think it is?"

"Yes, sir, I believe it is."

The image on the screen was of a spacecraft. A massive spacecraft.

The sensor information streaming along the bottom of the screen reported it was over five miles long and six miles wide. The hull was crimson red with a yellow lightning bolt emblazoned across the meteor-scarred plating.

The screen shimmered and the magnification brought the image of the ship in closer. As the image sharpened, he could make out more details along its pitted and battered hull.

Piper could now make out a series of letters in an alien language.

"Brain, can we translate that language?"

"Huh, yes, sir."

Now Piper was really worried. His stomach knotted with tension. This meant the language was one in the translator's memory core. Not good. We've seen these guys before.

I have a bad feeling about this.

"The words are a name," said The Brain.

"Go ahead." Piper held his breath. Please no....not on my watch.

"The name is Whiskey Bottle." Piper could hear the fear in The Brain's tone. A fear he shared. His heart was beating fast and a bead of sweat trickled down the side of his face. He knew the ramifications of such a name.

Oh, stub butts! They're back. The Lushites have returned!

Why does this stuff always happen to me?

Chapter One

"By the power vested in me, I name you smoker and smokee."
– Said by a priest of the Tobacco Leaf Order at the first legal wedding between a human and a cigarette, circa 4003

VICE PRESIDENT JALAPENO POPOVER THE TENTH, a short, skeletal man with a hairless, nut-brown head, beady black eyes, and bushy gray eyebrows, looked up from the tablet screen when the comm unit on his desk rang its familiar Galaxy Tobacco jingle chime. He detested being interrupted when studying the numbers for his beloved Galaxy Tobacco. Not that they ever changed. Always profits no losses, was the norm, but something had changed. For the first time in history they were leaking money

But where was the money going?

The red light blinked at the top of the rolling, paper-thin unit as it flashed on and off repeatedly accompanied by the lovely, yet equally annoying, shrill ring.

Jal leaned back in his faux leather executive chair and sighed, his left arm dropping to the arm of the chair. He set the cigar he'd been smoking in the onyx ashtray next to his right elbow and stared at the comm unit. His red-rimmed eyes sagged at the corners from lack of sleep.

He and the Brain had been at it for two weeks, and so far he'd found nothing amiss. There was zero evidence of a drain on the company accounts. GT was headed for financial ruin within two months if they didn't find the source of the leak soon. It wasn't like GT could go to the space cops.

Not that GT did all their business on the books but bringing in the official authorities was not an option. His mother's prophetic words returned from the back of his mind, "Reap the tobacco leaves you sow, you may have to sleep in them." He never understood much of what she said, but somehow these words seemed appropriate to this situation.

Now this call had interrupted him.

It had to be Mr. Roll Yer Own, the CEO and President of Galaxy Tobacco, calling to hear the results of his investigation. The CEO had been pounding his desk for weeks. He wanted the culprit found.

"Open comm," he said in a dull tone that belied his usual cheerful disposition.

"Sir. It's Pucker Bomb." A wave of relief washed over Jal as his security specialist's crimson face and pupiless, oil-black eyes appeared on the monitor. Pucker, from a race of four-armed, red-skinned, female humanoids, had been the security chief at GT for over two hundred years. Security was a tradition in her family that went back a minimum of fifteen hundred years. (Unsupported rumors said her family went back farther, but this had yet to be confirmed and Pucker wasn't talking.)

Her grandmother, Cherry Bomb, had even met his ancestor, Jal Popover the First, the co-founder of the new galactic order in the year 3333 and a 1/3.

It was hard for Jal to fathom a galaxy that lived on fast food. Fast food had been banned since the Day of The Great Smoke in 3333, when a big ball of garbage passed through the inhabited center of the galaxy.

After this upheaval, smoking became the vice of choice on Dirt. Smoking soon spread rapidly across the galaxy, helped along of a royal degree from the emperor. According to legend, Emperor Bud Wiser the First crushed any opposition to smoking like a spent cigarette butt, and brought the remaining star systems in line, with a mysterious power called The Slurp.

The official record stated the Emperor handpicked his Warriors of the Slurp to act as the guardians of the universe (mostly though to ensure the emperor's relatives both now and in the future kept their cushy jobs) for over 1000 years. That was until the warrior's mysterious disappearance while traveling to a smoker's conference on Filter Tipped II back in 4222. No one had seen the WOS in over two hundred years. In hindsight, renting a party star ship so all of your warriors could travel together to a distant uncharted star system was a definite mistake.

With the loss of his royal muscle, Bud Wiser XXII abdicated and disappeared into exile. It was generally believed the former emperor was hiding somewhere in the carbon nebula, but no one bothered to confirm this. Out of sight, out of mind was the new normal.

Jal was a practical man. He didn't believe in the so-called magical powers of the Slurp. As far as he was concerned it was superstition for the masses.

According to the legends, the WOS had mysterious powers, derived from their control of The Slurp, which they used to suck the brains out of their victims' ears. And it was said they could levitate tables, buildings, family pets, and even shift the orbits of planets (Really? Like someone would believe this crap? Really?) to scare systems into submission. Smokey mirrors, as far as Jal was concerned. He believed they used tricks and illusions to create these legends, and gullible fools decided they were real. Nonsense.

With no emperor, the tobacco corporation CEO's stepped in and took control of the galaxy. Now every planet, every star system, was property of one of the big six. But it wasn't all peace-pipes. Tensions had been rising between the multi-galactic corporations for decades to the point now where civil war seemed inevitable.

Jal thought the galaxy could use the distraction of a good external threat to take their minds off the impending tobacco war. The old slight of hand trick, he mused. "So what's up, Pucker?"

"I've received a message, sir, from Surveillance Outpost 3.103.243.9."

She paused, and he sensed something had made her nervous. Since nothing ever scared Pucker or made her nervous, whatever was bothering her had to be big. Now he was interested.

"What's the message?' He couldn't keep the excitement from his voice.

"It says simply, The Lushites have returned. Or so the comm officer who sent the message reported."

Jal froze and his heart skipped a beat. The Lushites? He scowled and his stomach muscles tightened. "Does it say anything else?" He spat the words from between gritted teeth. A surveillance station that far out must be staffed by a rookie, a crushed cigar butt of a humanoid no doubt.

"No, sir, that's all."

Moron. The surveillance officer better be green as raw tobacco. And most importantly he better be right or he would be more than fired, he'd be smoked. "What's the surveillance officers name?"

"Well, Jal — "

"That's Vice President Popover, Ms. Bomb."

"Yes, sir." Pucker's voice hardened and her eyes avoided his.

Jal's gray eyes narrowed and he rested his elbows on the plasti-steel desk in front of him and interlocked his fingers. His knuckles were white. He leaned toward the comm unit. "The officer's name?"

"The report was signed by the assistant to the assistant surveillance officer. His name is Piper Cleaner. Sir."

Jal's eyebrows shot up his forehead. A junior officer was on duty when the Lushite ship was detected. This could work to my advantage. "Was he alone?"

"Yes, sir."

"Okay. I get it. Put me in touch with him. I want a private comm link with Cleaner. And, Pucker..."

"Yes, sir?"

"Just in case this turns out to be something instead of the nothing I'm sure it is, make sure the link is encrypted." He eyed the pink-skinned security alien with one eyebrow arched. He coughed then cleared his throat and added, "Understood?"

"Yes, sir, understood. I'll have The Brain set up the link right away as you direct. It will be available in three minutes."

Three minutes? Some days he thought the Brain's response times were getting longer and longer, as if the Brain were purposefully blocking him. He better not be trying to undermine my authority. He filed a mental note to have Pucker look into The Brain's performance times and improve them. Pucker could be very persuasive.

Jal shrugged. Ultimately The Brain's time frame performance wasn't his problem. His job was tobacco consumer testing, not delivery target times.

He punched the button to cut off the conversation with Brain and snagged a cigar from the tray in the built-in arm of his chair. He stuck it in his mouth and ordered it lit.

A robotic arm appeared from a hidden panel that opened in the ceiling. The arm extended, and as it did a wooden match appeared in the articulated hand at the end of the arm. The thumb rested on the tip of the artificial wooden match. Real wood was too expensive even for executives. Besides the artificial wood was just as good as real wood, if not better.

The hand was constructed of a type of metal specially made for lighting matches. The thumb scratched across the match and it burst into flame.

The arm extended the yellow flame to the end of the cigar and settled on the tip. Jal began to puff gray-white smoke as the cigar's tip glowed a warm red.

"Thanks," said Jal. He loved being a vice president. The smoking' perks were awesome, and best of all tobacco was free to elected officials and paid employees of GT. Interns had to buy their own.

Jal sank back in the padded chair and watched the smoke disappear into the ceiling.

"Sir." It was The Brain on the comm. Pucker must have delegated the AI to the comm task. Jal glanced at the digital clock on the wall. Two minutes and forty-nine seconds. Things were looking up. It's gonna be a good day after all.

"Yes, Brain?"

"I have Assistant to the Assistant Surveillance Officer Cleaner on the horn."

"The horn?"

"Huh, sorry, sir I was watching ancient movie vids late last night and they use phrases like cell, telephone, blower, and horn when referring to comm systems."

Jal scowled. "Well I hate it. Don't do it again."

"Yes, sir."

"Never mind that particulate. We'll butt out about this later. Put on Cleaner. Now."

A shy, small voice echoed through the comm speaker. "Uhhh, it's me, Mr. President. Piper Cleaner. Sir."

Jal rolled his eyes. The Brain was a real pain in his butt, because he had him yelling comm at Cleaner over the comm link. He needed to know what Cleaner knew before anyone else at corporate. If this event turned out to be something then he had to be ready to take the credit. And ready to lay the blame. Either way, AACC Piper Cleaner was his man.

Jal forced a smile to his gaunt features. "Brain, put AACC Cleaner on the monitor in my office."

A thin male (whose age appeared to be south of twenty) appeared on the screen. Piper had sunken cheeks and a pale yellow pallor. His purple hair stuck straight up from his head as if it had been glued there.

Hmmm...handsome example of a Methanite. Doesn't look particularly bright which is a good thing. For me.

Jal puffed his cigar sending clouds of smoke into the air of his office. He grinned. "Hello, Piper. May I call you Piper?"

"Uuuh, yes, sir. Mr. President. Sir."

Jal wiggled the cigar sticking out of the side of his mouth. He chuckled. "Good. Though, Piper, I'm a vice-president not the president." One day. If this goes as planned, things will be very different, he thought.

He dropped his legs off his desk, clamped the cigar between his teeth and glared at the nervous officer on his screen.

Jal recognized nervous officers when sweat dripped off their chin as if a tap had been left open.

And leaving a dripping tap on at a deep space outpost would get you shoved out an airlock with the spent cigarette butts and ashes.[2]

Jal leaned in closer to the screen. He relished intimidating the junior officers. He smiled a tight, humorless smile like the one his father gave him when, at the age of five, he gave him his first pack of menthols. "So you say you spotted a Lushite ship, is this correct, Piper?"

Piper swallowed hard and his eyes flitted away from the screen for a millisecond then locked on his. The boy's lower lip trembled. "Huh, yes. I mean, yes sir."

Jal sat back in his chair twirled the cigar and puffed on it for several seconds. His beady eyes fixed on the boy's. Someone was coaching him. He wasn't alone. He thought for a moment it might be Him, but that wasn't possible. He hadn't been seen or heard from in years. Decades even. No, his clone wasn't anywhere near Surveillance Outpost 3.103.243.9, so who was off screen, guiding this lad?

Jal's brow formed into ridges. "So tell me how you know the ship your sensor picked up was a Lushite ship, and not some stray comet or rogue planet?"

The boy swallowed hard coughed then said, "I captured a long range image of the ship. Sir."

Jal extracted the smoking cigar from his mouth and placed it in the ashtray. "OK. Let's see it."

Piper's eyes flitted off the right again then back to him. "Yes, sir. I'll have The Brain bring it up immediately." He looked to his left at a consol. "Brain. Transmit the image to the Vice President."

"Which one?" said the Brain's voice.

---

2   *Note to reader: We agree, recycling of old butts and ashes is very important to us, too; but in deep space no one can hear you smoke so we had to toss them out with the trash. Sorry.*

Piper smiled sheepishly and his sunken cheeks flashed crimson. "Uhhh, Brain, the one on the comm screen right now."

"Uh, uh, and who is he when he's not in the smoking section?"

Piper's eyes widened. "Uhhh, sorry, Mr. Vice President, you know how Brains' can be."

Jal rolled his eyes. "Do I ever," he muttered.

"Sorry, sir, did you say something?"

The fear in Piper's eyes made Jal proud to be a vice president. "Never mind. Let me talk to your Brain." Piper nodded, uncertain what to do, folding and unfolding his hands in his lap.

"Brain?" said Jal.

"Yes, sir," came the reply through the surround sound speakers. His Brain somehow knew he wasn't talking to him. Good it made things simpler if you kept your Brains separate.

"Brain, listen closely." Jal paused then said, "Code green alpha-filter tip-lucky seven-two-one-roll-yer-own-yellow-eight."

"Yes, sir!" came the sharp, almost military-precise, immediate reply. The screen shimmered and there in the center of the screen was a football-shaped spacecraft. The scarred hull was a cherry red and there was a lemon yellow lightning bolt painted across the hull near the front (not that a front or back looked any different but Jal made the decision to call one end the front and other the back). Under the lightning bolt was elegant writing too small to clearly make out no matter how much he squinted.

Jal scratched at his right ear lobe absentmindedly. It could be Lushite, but he needed more proof. "Brain, magnify the writing."

The images shimmered and once it stopped the letters were large enough to read. Since his ancestors had made first contact with this species he had been taught to read their language.

Sure enough the name painted across the hull was clearly L.S.S. Whiskey Bottle a typical Lushite naming convention. At least that was what he'd read in the history file his father showed him before he forced him out of the company and assumed absolute control over the product delivery department of the galaxy-wide corporation.

The Lushites always named an object after a particular intoxicating beverage. Jal frowned and peered hard at the screen. Then he spotted it.

Under the ship's name was smaller print. As his father used to say, "If you want the truth always read the fine print."

"Brain, magnify another ten times and focus on the fine print under the ship's name." The image shimmered again.

When the image settled, Jal's jaw dropped open and he almost fell backward out of his chair. It was true. The Lushite Alliance had returned.

His heart beating hard in his chest, and without bothering to grab his half-smoked cigar or shut off his screen, he headed for the lift to the executive floor ten stories above. The president must be notified immediately. This could mean war.

On the screen were the words: PROPERTY OF THE LUSHITE ALLIANCE. HAVE A NICE DAY.

Chapter Two

"You are now on level three. You are a very poor excuse for a player. You should give up now, you worm."
–Hologame, The Worm Turns Five – Back for More Jack

CYBER DRIVE, DISGUISED AS HIS FAVORITE broad–shouldered, heavily-muscled avatar, studied the creature standing across the player grid from his avatar. He'd chosen the sword master because the red beast he faced, with its six-inch claws, mouth full of razor sharp teeth, and natural body armor was a difficult kill. He didn't want to fail. Killshot would never forget if he failed, and on a long, intergalactic trip such as this one a memory could be very long, indeed.

Cy withdrew the seven-foot long sword from the scabbard on his avatar's hip and tensed the character's heavily muscled arms. Gritting his teeth, he waited for the inevitable attack. The creature was breathing hard now and snorting from its nostrils trying to clear its nasal passages. It seemed winded; a quick glance at the energy level of his opponent confirmed the creature had lost half its energy.

A slow, crooked smile formed on his avatar's lips. After sweeping his long, thick, black, shoulder-length hair back on his head with his free hand, he raised the sword higher, gripping the leather-wrapped hilt with both strong, rough hands.

This is gonna be fun. He'd finally beat Killshot at a game. He could feel the excitement building in his stomach.

He grabbed the can of Blast from the holder in his chair arm and took a long drag of the super high-energy drink. His heart rate increased and his head pounded for several seconds before his bodily systems adjusted to the sudden adrenaline rush.

Since they left their home star system five years ago, he had yet to beat her at any of the sixteen million hologames in the database (they'd only played sixteen hundred and three so far). He'd hoped to complete twenty thousand sessions before they arrived in the fast food galaxy. But alas he would have to settle for where they were.

"Brain, how long until we reach Dirt?"

"Six days ship's time," Brain replied his voice betraying a sense of uncertainty.

Cyber paused, and on the player grid his avatar lowered his arms slightly, also lowering the sword.

Suddenly, with a deep roar the red beast leapt at him. The enraged beast slammed hard into Cyber's avatar, forcing it to stumble backward until it fell onto its back with a ragged cry of rage. Through the avatar's eyes he saw the red beast fly over him, its fangs glistening, its razor tipped claws extended. The beast could have killed his avatar. No doubt Killshot knew she had the advantage and decided to tease him like a kitten with a string. He'd made the mistake of confiding in KS about his favorite childhood came called Kitten On A String. No doubt KS knew this would touch a nerve with him. Some days she really made him a Pissed Pistofferson.

A glance at his avatar's energy gauge confirmed the attack had drained seventy five percent of his remaining energy. Cyber frowned. *What a wanker I am.* A momentary distraction may have cost him the first game he had a shot at winning against his oldest foe.

Jack it. If I want to win now I'd have to use my remaining reserve power.

He'd been hoping to save the reserve for the final battle, but he either used it now or he'd lose this level and there would be no final battle. Unless he got lucky and struck a fatal blow before his power died. Only it wasn't worth the effort. Not now. But someday he'd make KS pay for her arrogance.

As was his habit he adjusted the mike attached to the headband so the sensitive microphone was closer to his mouth. "Killshot, are you jacked in?" he said.

"Yeah, I'm here. Loser."

Cyber winced. "Listen, I'll retire the match to you if you don't destroy my 'tar. Agreed?"

Killshot was silent for several seconds then she sighed and agreed to his terms. Game etiquette required a player to accept an opponent's surrender gracefully; if she didn't, the game's Brain would assess demerit points based on a totally random algorithm. Killshot could end up with so many demerits she'd automatically lose the next hundred games. Like any expert gamer, Killshot loved to win. Losing was not an option, so she would accept his surrender.

"Good. Thanks." Cyber then shut off the hologrid and rose from his player chair. As he did the chair retracted and disappeared into a hole that opened in the floor. It closed as Cyber exited the pod.

Cyber walked to the refrigerator standing against one wall of the player deck.

The room was oval-shaped and there were sixty stations lining the wall interrupted by the refreshment zone that boasted a fridge, microwave (for popcorn, of course), and a sink to wash your hands in after a particularly intense game. Fingers could get sooo sweaty.

The ship was on auto-intergalactic travel so no sentient being was needed to steer. The onboard AI (known as The Brain) would keep the vessel on course until they arrived at their predetermined destination.

Cyber took out a cold can of Blast from the fridge and popped the top. There was a satisfying hiss as the preserved air in the can was released. The licorice odor wafted over him, flaring his nostrils and tickling his pleasure center. Cy closed his eyes and emitted a deep sigh. There was nothing better than a cold can of Blast. Unless, of course you counted a game win. If there was one thing the Lushite Alliance did right, though they were often too drunk to realize it, was they were really good at developing beverages that offered a complete sensory experience.

When they loaned the LSS Whisky Bottle to the Gamers League there was only one condition: they had to find out what happened to crew of the LSS Shot. According to President Harvey Wallbanger of the Lushite Alliance, they hadn't received so much as a text message in over a thousand years and they were beginning to be concerned. Not that Harvey was all that reliable, but Cyber believed him when he said they hadn't heard from the Shot in a while.

No one became concerned when an intergalactic Lushite ship went missing for seven or eight hundred years. The majority of the Lushite Alliance fleet was spread all over the universe, after all. Travel in hyperspace often meant generations would go by before any one ship seemed gone for too long. And since there were a lot of bars along the way, and no Lushite would pass up a new watering hole, long stops at a new bar were not unusual.

The Shot's mission had been to follow up on reports of a new bar in the Pretzel Nebula two galaxies over and report back. The last message said they had made a wrong turn and were stopping at another galaxy along their route, and they had not been heard from since.

Cyber and his crew were headed for a major gaming convention two galaxies over when they encountered the trail of dead soldiers from the Shot.[3]

The cans and bottles were labeled PROPERTY OF THE LSS SHOT. This discovery led them into the galaxy ahead and slightly to the right of their original course. Since it wasn't much out of their way, it wouldn't be too much trouble to make a quick stop and remind the Shot's crew to call home. Cyber decided to alter their flight plan slightly and look for the Shot on the way home after the convention.

Cyber looked up at the massive view screen that covered the wall in front of him from one end of the player deck to the other. The screen displayed all sorts of data, such as available air, snack food inventory reports, number of cans of Blast in stock…all the important stuff. Cyber was relieved to see a report that stated the supply hold still contained at least five decades worth of all the major food groups; potato chips, candy, caramel corn, and freezer ice pops.

There was also a continuous track line in the trademarked lime green of Ziggy's Warrior Butts on a universal map, showing the current position of the ship from their point of origin to their destination. A blinking digital display in the top right of the map showed the elapsed time to their destination.

---

3   *Note to reader: For the uninitiated, "dead soldiers" usually, but not always, refers to empty cans and/or bottles that used to contain alcohol-based beverages.*

The robo-probes sent ahead to follow the Lushite empties were leading them to a small insignificant planet called Dirt located on one of this galaxy's spiral arms. According to the Brain, Dirt was the home planet of a race of fast foodies who ruled this galaxy. At least they were the last time the available data was updated about this galaxy more than one thousand years ago, local time. Who knew what had happened there since then? Not even the Brain was willing to speculate in that regard. He'd been burned too many times when making what he called educated guesses, which turned out quite naturally to be wild-ass guesses.

There was the time he guessed the final battle scenario in Battle of the Bloodworms. That guess had resulted in the loss of a ship and an elite gaming crew to a rookie crew in the galactic finals. No wonder the Brain had been reluctant to make any wild guesses since.

Cyber raised the can to his lips, took a long swig and shivered as the immediate rush hit his system. He gazed at the blinking light on the map, and wondered if Dirt had changed.

He shrugged. What did he care?

He turned away, heading toward the lift that would deliver him to his game pod. He had a four-hour sleep cycle coming he was looking forward to, and he needed to be plugged in if he was going to be able to sleep. He'd been plugged in since he was a year old, which he always thought made so much sense. How else would you raise children? Like duhhhh....

Not that he would have any kids. Sure he'd met some cool game babes in the virtual universe, but he'd never met one in person long enough to have kids. The real world sucked most of the time.

As the lift door closed and he felt the mild increase in gravity as the car sped between decks, he dismissed any thought of concern.

They had six days to gather more data before they arrived at the fast food planet.

Besides what was the worst that could happen?

***

When Cyber woke from his sleep game, he nearly jumped out of his crimson skin. A large white eyeball, about five feet in circumference, with a bright green iris was hovering over the see-through pod door, staring at him through the glass. "Hey! Brain! What are you doing outside my pod!"

After pausing the sleep game he spoke the verbal command, "Pod, open." The pod door swung open and Cyber stepped out. He stretched his long, lean arms over his head and scratched his belly. "Brain, why are you in my pod bay? And why did you appear as that stupid eye hologram? You know I hate that thing." Unblinking eyeballs creeped him out.

"Sorry, Cyber, but I needed to see you right away and the eyeball holo seemed appropriate."

Cyber studied the eyeball hologram for any signs the AI was being funny, but single eyeballs are difficult to read for body language, so he had no idea. "OK, for now. What's so important you'd interrupt my sleep gaming?"

"We received a message."

Jack it, Cyber thought, a message from anyone usually meant bad news. No way he could avoid this so he decided he might as well hear whatever whoever had to say. He took a sip from the warming Blast can in his hand then used the can to point to the monitor covering most of the wall in the game pod bay.

"Where's the message from?"

"From a monitoring outpost at the edge of the galaxy .5732 light years off the starboard bow."

Hmmm, the fast food galaxy had detected their presence and was making first contact, thought Cyber. Interesting. Too bad it wasn't a data pack from home with the new game releases; but if this went well, they might get some first class snack foods.

"Let's see it," he said.

The holo-eyeball floated away from him moving closer to the wall monitor. As the AI's surrogate moved away, the monitor flickered and a grainy image began to coalesce on the screen.

"Can't you clean it up, Brain?"

"Sorry, but for reasons I'm unable to determine, the image is far less than optimal."

"I know that, genius. Tell me if you can fix it."

"No," replied The Brain with no further explanation. Cyber thought he heard an edge in the AI's tone that suggested it was annoyed or even frustrated. How odd, he thought, AI's never get frustrated, it isn't in their programming, or so I've been told. This could be very exciting.

Cyber squinted at the screen. The image had cleared enough so he could see a vaguely humanoid shape, which was a relief. If had been a shapeless blob, or a giant insect, communication would have been even more difficult than it was likely to be already. He hoped the interstellar translator could understand it, him, or her.

"Hello?" he said to the image. "Can you hear me?"

"Hey, who's there?" said a feminine voice. At least the translator made whoever it was sound feminine, and thankfully she spoke galactic.[4]

4   Note to reader: Galactic is an amalgamation of all the languages used by all species on the inhabited worlds in the Milky Way galaxy. The adoption of a single galactic language was made official in 2665, at the end of the Franchise Wars, by the First Republic Assembly.

"This is Cyber Drive captain of the LSS Whisky Bottle whom am I addressing?"

Static. Then a garbled voice said something too distorted for him to make out.

"Say again," said Cyber. His stomach muscles knotted. He needed to get back to gaming. This interruption was taking wayyyy too long. The game was on pause but his muscled thumbs were already beginning to itch for action.

"Sorry," said the female voice much clearer this time. "I had to make some adjustments to the signal processor. Anyway, as I was saying my name is Smokey Cigarillo, I'm looking for the emperor. Please put him on the linn."

Cyber's hands began to shake and his cheeks grew cold. Emperor Wiser? This woman knows the despot of Beer Pong V? "Uhhh, you see, uhhhh..." I'm sounding like an idiot. "Sorry, it's kind of a shock to meet someone in another galaxy who knows Emperor Wiser. I mean he's certainly famous where I'm from (or should I say infamous), but here in the fast food galaxy?" Cyber chuckled uneasily and shifted his feet back and forth like a hatchling that needed to use the toilet. A burst of laughter erupted from the figure on the comm screen startling him. "What's so funny?" asked Cyber.

After several seconds the laughter finally subsided. "I'm not laughing at you, Captain Drive. I should explain. According to the history logs, and these records are from more than a thousand years ago, local time, the navigator of the LSS Shot made a wrong turn while on the way to the Pretzel Nebula and entered this galaxy. That navigator was Bud Wiser.

"After a series of unfortunate events, the galaxy's system of government changed and Wiser and a mail boy named Jalapeño Popover founded a church dedicated to tobacco and smoking."

Cyber shook his head. "No, that can't be right, the emperor returned from this galaxy by hijacking the L.S.S. Plonk, accompanied by a vicious warrior named J. Cheesy Popover. Together they overthrew the Lushite Alliance and replaced it with the Gamers Alliance who rules our galaxy to this day. Fortunately the remaining Lushites rent their fleet of intergalactic ships for booze cruises and other social events."

Finally the screen cleared and the fuzzy image coalesced into the angular features of a nut-brown skinned woman with almond-shaped eyes. Between her full, red lips was a long brown stick, the tip of which trailed a thin stream of white smoke. Behind her was a window overlooking a cityscape filled with spires of tall buildings. Her generous mouth had formed an easy grin with one side of her mouth curled slightly upward; her dark eyes seemed to sparkle with amusement. "What social event made you rent the Whisky Bottle?"

"We're on our way to a gaming convention at Epsilon X and just wanted to make a short stop to remind the crew of the Shot to call home. We haven't heard from them in a while."

Smokey took a drag on her thin stick and then blew a smoke ring. She chuckled. "You mean the ancestors of the Shot's crew, right?"

Cyber had to think about that for a moment. Time wasn't relative in intergalactic travel so Smokey's question seemed absurd. "I'm sorry, Smokey, I assume it's okay to call you Smokey?" She nodded her agreement so Cyber continued, "You can call me Cyber by the way. Anyway, I'm confused. The crew should still be alive. Since time is compressed during intergalactic travel, they should only be a few years older than when they left our galaxy."

The grin disappeared from Smokey's angular features replaced by a frown that now marred her smooth forehead. "I'm sorry as well, I assumed you knew.

The Shot's crew arrived here one thousand years ago. They have been dead for several hundred years."

Cyber eyed the female alien. If what she said was true this could mean war. Not holo-war in a gamers' universe, but real war in the real universe with real death and real destruction.

Cyber's hands slowly curled into fists and his hearts began to beat faster. And I'm just the being to start the ball rolling. After all I'm a level one hundred master battle troll who kicks butt as part of a regular fitness regime.

Chapter Three

"Game over."
–The final words of Marking Time, Captain of the Gamers Research vessel, Move It Or Lose It, before it disappeared into a black hole.

SMOKEY WAVED HER HANDS after stubbing out her smoking stick in a glass tray on the desk in front of her. Still the heavenly odor of burnt tobacco filled her senses. "No, no, Cyber, you've got the wrong idea. We didn't kill them. They abandoned their ship and joined our society after the Day of the Big Smoke." The irises of Cyber's pink eyes narrowed. Smokey could see the doubt in the alien's expression. Funny thing about aliens, humans, and other more exotic life forms, is doubt is the one universal expression they all share.

"Listen, I'm not an expert on history but I do know Bud Wiser never left Dirt a thousand years ago so whoever came back to your galaxy it wasn't Wiser," she explained

Cyber's jowly features relaxed. "Really?" The alien Gamers' forehead wrinkled. "That's funny." His skin was the color of a sunbather who wore no sunscreen on a summer's day when the UV index was high, his hair reminded her of dried straw.

His red-rimmed eyes peering back at her through the view screen were watchful and alert. The bags of loose skin under his eyes made her wonder of these beings had sleep sickness – as in lack thereof.

"What's so funny? I assure you I'm not laughing," said Smokey.

Cyber shook his head. "If what you're saying is true, then the warrior J. Cheesy Popover might have been the power behind the throne for a fake Bud Wiser. It means the centuries we were ruled by the Wiser dynasty was a fraud, a deception greater than any ever perpetrated."

Smokey averted her gaze from the screen. He was right. But if the Wiser who returned to the Lushite Alliance wasn't their Bud Wiser then who was he? Her oil-black eyes flitted back to the monitor. "You know, captain there might be someone who might know the truth."

Cyber arched one eyebrow. "Really? Who?"

"Wiser's descendant is the former Emperor Bud Wiser XXII who at one time also ruled this galaxy."

"Really?" His eyes were wide and his voice now had an edge of excitement. Members of the Wiser dynasty ruled the two galaxies. "And where will we find him?"

Smokey frowned. "I'm not sure. He's in exile. We have another republic now." She rolled her eyes. "A so-called democracy." Cyber appeared quizzical. Smokey forced a smile onto her lips. "Sorry, not everyone likes the democratic process. Never mind that; I'll explain later. Right now we have to make contact with Vice President Popover on Dirt."

"Popover? I thought you said J. Cheesy Popover left your galaxy with our fake emperor."

Smokey chuckled uneasily. "No, no, I know this is confusing, but Jal Popover isn't the one you know as J. Cheesy..." Smokey paused. Was she really sure? "Jal and I were raised together.

We are both descendants of the original Smokey and Jal from the 34th century. I, too, am seeking answers to all this, and I hope Jal can help us."

Even on the monitor Cyber seemed to look through her. "You know, Smokey, if we determine this Jal is the same person as J. Cheesy it means—"

Smokey held up one hand. "War, yes I know. Frankly, I don't think that's in the best interests of either of our galaxies." She took in a deep breath to steady herself then said, "I'm on Surveillance Outpost 3.103.240.8. My Brain will send you the coordinates of the outpost. Come by and pick me up, and we'll go to Dirt together to meet Jal."

"Did you say you have a Brain?" Smokey nodded. "Not The Brain?" Smokey nodded again. Cyber's features were split by a wide grin. "Well what do you know? Wiser brought a Brain to our galaxy. We have them, too."

The Brain on Cyber's ship had been listening quietly until now. "I'm not a piece of furniture. As everyone knows AI's have feelings. You shouldn't talk about me as if I'm not in the room."

"Sorry, Brain..." Cyber and Smokey said in unison followed immediately by gales of laughter.

"Yeah, like this is going to go well," The Brain spoke softly so Cyber and Smokey couldn't hear him.

***

Two weeks local time, after the LSS Whiskey Bottle picked up Smokey at the surveillance outpost, they were soon back up to light speed plus three headed for planet Dirt, the home world of the alien calling herself Smokey Cigarillo. The trip would take a month, ship's time, six days local time. (Don't ask, time and space are just weird.)

Since the outpost was located on a spiral arm on the opposite side of the galaxy from the arm where Dirt was located. Cyber was secretly pleased the trip would take time; he wanted to know more about the details of these beings interactions with the Lushites.

Cyber eased back in an enveloper chair in the gamers' lounge and took a generous sip from a fresh can of Blast. He and Smokey were the only two beings in the lounge right now. The other tables were empty, though the snack bowls remained half full and the soda and energy drink dispensers that lined the pale yellow walls were still fully stocked. Like the walls of all of the buildings on his home world the shade of pale yellow comforted him. It reminded him of simpler times when he was a child, when he would blend into a wall to hide while playing hide and seek with his nest mates.

His eyes were watchful as he studied Smokey, carefully seated across from him in an identical enveloper chair. She was an interesting and beautiful female in person, even more so than on an interspace communication monitor. "So how long have you been at the outpost?" he asked his guest.

Smokey hadn't accept his offer of a can of Blast or an energy drink, but had nibbled on a few spiced Satay chips from the bowl on the table separating them. She seemed uneasy, nervous as if she would start biting her pale green nails at any moment.

"You appear uncomfortable," said Cyber after swallowing the cold, sugary Blast and feeling the immediate rush as it entered his bloodstream, "Is everything OK?"

Smokey's eyes flitted to his and she smiled shyly. Her cheeks reddened. Cyber didn't know what this meant; he still had a lot to learn about the Smokers, as she referred to her race. "I've never been on a Lushite vessel before and I'm a teeny bit afraid."

Cyber grinned. "Oh, there's nothing to worry about. Lushites vessels have been traveling between galaxies for tens of thousands of years and none have failed to transport their passengers and crews safely."

The Smoker woman nodded. "I'm sure what you say is true, but our history mentions a ship called a Flash-O-Matic 3000 that broke the dimensional barrier and disappeared from this reality."

The grin faded from Cyber's jowly, pale yellow features and his eyes narrowed. "I know something of this event."

Smokey shifted her shapely bottom forward to the edge of her chair and looked into Cyber's eyes. Her hands pressed into the faux leather arms of the chair causing the sensitive shaper molecules in the chair's mem-leather to reconfigure to match the contour of her fingers. "What do you know...exactly?"

"Peter and Trixie Pug arrived in our galaxy three years ago, local time. They currently reside on a planet called Snackcakes III, but they can be here in three months if need be."

Smokey appeared to think about Cyber's words for several seconds then said, "Yes, I think they should be welcomed home, but I have to clear it with Vice President Popover."

"Fair enough. The Brain will show to the communications center so you can call home." Cyber waved at The Brain who had remained in the single eyeball holo projection. "I'm going back to my game pod. I'll see you in a few days. Enjoy every amenity the ship has to offer. Try a game if you wish. I'm sure Brain can set you up with a game pod."

Smokey offered him a tight smile. "Thanks, I'll call home first."

"As you wish." Cyber stood and walked away leaving Smokey alone in the lounge.

After he entered the corridor leading to the lift shafts he stopped and activated the comm unit set into the wall and called for Brain.

The unit's monitor lit up and the image on the screen was of a white eyeball with a crimson iris. Cyber decided not roll his own eyes because it was creepy enough to be talking to the holo image Brain had chosen. He was a stubborn child when it came to be told what to wear and he didn't need to encourage his stubbornness.

"What's up, dude?" said the Brain.

'My name's Captain Drive, not dude. Use my proper name and title, Brain."

"Uhhh, sorry cap'n, those late night vids, man they mess with my head, know what I mean?"

"Yeah, right. Just knock it off." He sighed. "Never mind that crap, I want you to keep an eye — and no, it's not a pun — on Smokey and report back to me what she and that Jalapeño guy on Dirt talk about. I need Intel and I need to bad. We might be walking into a trap."

"Aren't we traveling faster than light in interstellar space? I don't believe walking is possible at these speeds and highly impract—"

"Shut up, Brain, you know perfectly well what I mean. Now I'm going to my game pod. I expect a full report in three days." Cyber walked away muttering under his breath about what a pain in the butt an AI can be.

"Geez, man," said The Brain, "some guys just have no sense of humor."

***

Smokey sat in the high backed swivel at the comm station. Affixed to the wall in front of her was a wide screen for face-to-face communication. She studied the controls. There were a series of colorful buttons with mushroom-shaped tops in avocado green, banana yellow, cherry red, and royal blue.

And one was black with an indecipherable word in large block letters above it console she assumed meant don't touch. And she certainly wouldn't touch any of them without knowing what each button did. For all she knew the black one might be the self-destruct button. Why a comm system would have a self-destruct button she had no idea, but she wasn't about to take any chances.

The Brain's white eyeball with the pink iris holo-image hovered over her left shoulder as if the AI were watching her. Brain AI's were apparently common throughout the galaxy, but this one somehow gave her a sense of unease, and she didn't know why.

"Brain, how does this comm system work?"

"Do you know the frequency of Dirt's interspace comm net?" asked the AI.

"Yes, it's alpha-six one two three."

"Kind of simple isn't it?"

Smokey swallowed a snort. She'd been saying the same thing to Jal for years but he said their Brain told him it was fine. As long as Brain liked something the way it was, so did Jal. "I agree, Brain, but your counterpart stated otherwise."

The Gamers' Brain made an odd trilling sound, which her Brain had never done, then said, "I'm looking forward to meeting this other Brain."

"I'm sure you are, but first I need to contact the VP, so if you cold please tell me how this thing works."

"Of course. I have made the adjustment to the frequency to match your comm net, so all you need to do now is slap the green button with the flat of your hand and you will be in contact immediately with your vice-president."

Smokey eyed the eyeball. Was it possible for a Brain to pull your leg? They were a long way from Dirt in this remote section of the galaxy, so communication tended to take time. Even with the latest version of the comm net, it took two days for a response. A real time conversation was impossible. But was it? The Lushite ship travelled at greater speed than anything in the Marketeer fleet, so their technology was clearly more advanced. It made sense they'd have a more efficient comm system.

Smokey reached out with her palm open hovering over the button, and hesitated. This might explode the ship, or perhaps unleash a terrible weapon, or release deadly gas into the atmosphere, was it worth the risk? She shook her head. Even the Lushites wouldn't blow up their own ship. Smokey slapped the button and immediately the screen on the wall in front of her lit up, shimmered, and she stared wide-eyed at Vice President Jal Popover seated behind his executive desk, the vice-presidential seal of office on a plasti-steel plaque on the wall behind him.

His expression was reminiscent of a vampire worm caught in the headlights of a space cruiser. He stared slack-jawed back at her, his mouth hanging open. "Smokey? How...? I mean..." He cleared his throat and stuck two fingers in the collar of the suit jacket that he always wore too tight for comfort.

"I'm sorry to interrupt you, Mr. Vice President, but I have important news, very important," Smokey blurted.

The short bald man seemed to gather himself quickly after the initial shock of real-time communication. Smokey was often surprised at how quickly politicians could regain their composure. He adjusted his lean frame in his executive chair and plucked a cigarette from the auto-dispenser in the drawer to his right.

He brought the fresh cigarette to his lips and a robotic arm extended from the top of the screen. The fingers on the end of the arm held a flame, which it used to light the tip of Jal's smoke. The smoke filled his nostrils after he puffed once, then he took a deep drag and eased back against the chair. His dark eyes locked on hers.

"Obviously, Smokey, I have a few questions." He paused to take in a fresh drag and the tip of his smoke glowed red. "But since you have important news, tell me that first." His tone was arrogant yet his body language said otherwise.

He might appear confident to the casual observer but she knew him better than anyone. His fingers were nervously playing with the cigarette, constantly shifting it around and using his thumb to push at the filtered end. Jal was scared; she recognized the look in his eyes. She'd seen the fear in his eyes before during their days together as space soldiers in the Grand Fleet of the New Republic.

"The Lushite vessel is carrying representatives of the Gamers Alliance. They rented this ship from the Lushites."

Jal arched one bushy eyebrow. "So we're not under attack? Things are bad enough without that. Thanks for the good news, tell them—"

Smokey interrupted him before Jal finished. "They're sending Peter and Trixie Pug back to us."

Jal's face paled and the hand holding the cigarette began to tremble. "The Pug's were lost over a thousand years ago." His voice was low and hoarse almost a whisper.

Smokey shook her head and adjusted her bottom on the chair. She sensed the gamers Brain nearby listening to this conversation. She wasn't stupid, the AI would tell Cyber everything they were saying, of that she was certain. "You-know-who will not be happy if they return."

Jal's eyes flitted away from the screen and he nodded. He took another hit of his cigarette then said; "Tell them we'd welcome Peter and Trixie with open arms."

"But, Mr. Vice President—" she began to protest before he cut her off.

"Just tell them." He swiveled his chair to face the monitor, his eyes serious and his nervousness gone. Jal scowled. "And tell them I look forward to their arrival on Dirt."

"Uhhh, yes, sir." Jal's image flickered then the screen went dark.

"Interesting fellow," said the Gamer's AI.

Smokey nodded. "Yeah, he's a real pip off the game board."

"I know a game that uses pips," said the Brain.

Smokey turned her chair and looked at the holo eyeball. She couldn't tell if the AI was joking, but she suspected he was serious. She decided to let the comment slide for now. Brains could be punsters but this one was from another galaxy, so she couldn't yet read it and didn't want to assume anything. "Listen, Brain, I'm hungry and could use a smoke. Is there somewhere onboard where I could get a bite to eat and have a cigarette?"

"Sure. No problem. When Captain Drive said we were picking up a smoker, I converted one of the old unused Lushite drinking lounges into a smokers lounge. They have a hotdog food dispenser and plenty of ashtrays. And an array of fully stocked cigarette machines. It's on deck 233A."

"Really?" Smokey chuckled. "No matter the galaxy, you Brains seem to think of everything."

"Yes, I know," replied the AI.

"And you're modest." The AI didn't respond. Smokey smirked to herself. "Maybe while I eat and smoke you can tell me all about the galaxy you come from?" she said.

"Certainly, the captain instructed me to provide all hospitality all the time. And I like to be in full compliance."

Smokey stood and started toward the row of lifts along the rear wall of the comm deck. "Brain, I think this the beginning of a beautiful friendship."

Chapter Four

"Hey, buddy can I bum a smoke?"
–Dirt Ambassador Benson at the first meeting with President Hedges of Morris V.

JAL GRIMACED WHEN the screen went dark. The communication had to be a fake, a trick by you-know-who. No one could send a live transmission from the other side the galaxy; it just wasn't possible. But this might be the answer to his dreams. A good old-fashioned revolution would solve all his problems. Of course, he'd execute anyone who stood in his way of his imperial plans. The president of GT would be the first to go, then the board of directors, then his fellow vice presidents. All that mocking deserved retaliation. The one wild card that concerned him was Admiral Awesome. Sure, he was a tool in the plan to take over the galaxy, but he may have plans of his own. He hoped Piper had found his royal rival on Four and eliminated him. You-know-who still had some loyal followers in the darker corners of some of the remote worlds controlled by GT.

The rebels might even rise up if He were to return from exile. Piper better get the job done, because if he failed Jal would have to depend on Smokey. And he hated the idea of owing her anything. If he looked up in the definition of the word "conniving" in the galactic dictionary, he fully expected to find her picture. Once he was crowned emperor, Smokey would have to go as well.

Jal stubbed out his cigarette in the ashtray Brain had materialized on his desk and retrieved his pipe from his shirt pocket. The pipe had an auto-beaming feature so that he didn't need to replenish the tobacco, even with heavy use, and he frequently used it for several hours a day. The built in lighter lit the tobacco in the bowl as soon as he raised the pipe to his lips.

The smokey, rum-flavored weed filled his nostrils and mouth; he couldn't help smiling at the heady aroma. He closed his eyes and hummed a few bars of his favorite song. Pipe smoking had always been such a soothing pastime.

"Brain," he said finally breaking his silence, "find Admiral Awesome. Tell him I need to see him immediately." Pausing to consider his next words he added, "Also, tell him it's a category Viceroy-Six emergency." V-six was the category just short of all out war, so Admiral A should be in his office very quickly.

"But, Mr. Vice President, I don't think a VP is permitted to designate that particular threat level," pointed out Brain. He was right of course; only the president, or the make-war-not-peace cabinet, could start an argument between worlds, Vice Presidents were only allowed to advise the galaxy of threatening shortages of marshmallows or animal crackers or if there was an impending ecological threat of tobacco crop failure on some of the member worlds in the Tobacco Fields Coalition. But since his goal was to gain the admiral's attention, it should do the trick.

"Just send the message, Brain."

"OK," replied the AI, "it's your funeral." After a two-second pause, Brain spoke again. "The admiral will be here in three minutes."

Right on cue, the teleporter pad began to glow and the tall, muscular form of Admiral Reel Awesome shimmered into existence on the pad, dressed in his usual ivory white dress uniform, his wide shoulders dripping with gold epaulets. His barrel chest brimmed with combat medals and campaign ribbons– all honorary, because though he was commander of the Grand Fleet, and had graduated first in his senior officers class at the Academy some two hundred years before, he'd never so much as fired a pulse rifle in anger, or even by accident.

Jal noted the Admiral's complexion was somewhere between the color of red wine grapes and a summer apple. He was beyond angry. As expected, once the teleporter had completed transport, the Admiral stormed off the pad. His fists were clenched, and his knuckles were white as hot ash.

"Mr. Vice President! This is an outrage!" he began, launching into a far more colorful use of verbiage. The number of spine-twisting sexual positions he suggested Jal partake of was truly impressive. Jal thought he could almost see smoke coming from the irate officer's ears. Not that smoking ears was all that uncommon, but he knew the Admiral preferred stogies to ear smokes.

Jal watched the angry admiral in silence for several minutes, all the while puffing silently on his wooden pipe. Finally, when the Admiral ran out of curses, he stopped talking. Breathing hard, he collapsed into the chair across the desk from Jal.

"Brain," said Jal, "get the Admiral a cup of leaf tea."

"Tea for two?" asked Brain. Jal nodded.

Jal regarded the Admiral in silence for several more seconds. Lowering his pipe, he said, "Admiral, I needed you here because you and I share a common problem."

The admiral scowled at him. "That's impossible. You and I have nothing in common. You're an accountant, I'm a warrior."

Jal chuckled. "You're as much a bean counter as I am, admiral. I know all about those rerouted cigar shipments from Cuba IV to your home world. Cuban cigars are still illegal on some worlds are they not?"

Admiral Awesome glared at Jal. "Of course they are. And I know nothing about any diversions of Cubans."

"Really?" Jal chuckled, again puffing on his pipe.

The admiral pulled a cigarette pack from a pocket inside his uniform jacket and tapped out a cigarette. A lighter appeared in his other hand and soon he had the tip glowing red and had taken a deep drag on the filtered end. He blew a cloud of smoke into the air. The air filters cleaned away the whiskey-soaked smoke within milliseconds.

"Do you know a Commander Camel?" The Admiral's face sagged and his eyes widened.

"How do you know him?"

"Camel works for me. He's my inside man on your command ship."

The ridges on the Admiral's brow grew more pronounced as his scowl deepened and his puffy cheeks became a shade of purple. "How dare you," he sputtered, spittle shooting from his mouth.

Jal wondered if he might have finally pushed the decorated officer too far. Not that it worried him in particular, but he needed the Admiral's cooperation if his plan to take over the galaxy was to succeed. Jal chuckled as the Admiral lit another cigarette after stubbing out the first one in the ashtray.

"Take it easy, admiral, I have spies everywhere. You're not so unique as to have earned any special attention." Jal reached for the oak humidor on the desk next to his statue of Cigar Man, the fictional superhero mascot of Galaxy Tobacco. He flipped open the lid and offered the Admiral a cigar from his private stock of Cubans from Fidel II, the finest and most expensive cigars in the galaxy.

The Admiral, never one to turn down a fine cigar, accepted one and ran it under his nose, taking a deep intake of the aroma. His eyes closed, his bulky frame visibly relaxed, and his shoulders drooped. Fine tobacco could be a natural sedative. No wonder smoking had spread so rapidly after the Great Smoke.

"Now perhaps you and I can discuss the reason I asked for you," said Jal.

The Admiral of the Grand Fleet's eyes snapped opened and he eyed the vice-president suspiciously. "Why would you use such an illegal ruse to get me here?"

Jal eased back in his executive chair, the cushions comfortable under his butt, and grinned. "Oh, come now, admiral, we've both done some things outside the law to get where we are today. What I'm proposing is we team up to take over the galaxy. We'd share the spoils 50-50." Like his father often said, "When you need an ally, always appeal to their greed."

The Admiral's eyebrows rose simultaneously. He reached for the large lighter on Jal's desk and, after biting off the tip of one end, lit the cigar. He puffed until the tip glowed red and a trail of fragrant, dark, rum-scented smoke rose into the air. "OK, let's supposed we could do this. Why do I need you? I have the fleet. All you have is a few strategic spies and a minor position in the government. My fleet could take over without a politician, and, frankly, we'd be better off without your types."

"Except I have information that benefits us both. An ally who will send the galaxy into chaos once the news leaks. And a potential ally that could help us to seize power when the government collapses under civil unrest."

Awesome nodded. Jal knew he had the decorated military leader right where he wanted him. "Really? And who is the ally?" said Awesome, his shifting in his chair evidence of his struggle to contain his excitement from his voice.

"The Lushites have returned."

***

An hour later, Jal sat alone in his apartment overlooking the hazy city, which was spread out before him, like an island floating on a carpet of puffy clouds. The diffused sunlight that managed to cut through the smoke from the smoking factories gave the gray clouds a glowing beauty that forced a grin of appreciation onto the vice-president's lips. He brought a cigarette to his lips and took a deep drag. The smoke tasted good and the tension in his shoulders and neck eased slightly. Releasing the smoke from his lungs he sighed and moved away from the windows, going to the desk in his home office.

"Do you think Awesome will keep his part of the agreement?" said Brain.

Jal sat in the padded chair behind the wide, clear plasti-steel desk. "I expect he'll double cross me."

"Then why did you tell him about the Lushites?"

Jal smirked. "What did I tell him, exactly?"

The Brain remained silent. Jal knew why. He hadn't really told Awesome much of anything. Not that he had his spy, Smokey Cigarillo, on their ship right now and that he was about to dispatch Piper Cleaner on a suicide mission to destroy the Lushite vessel.

Once this attack succeeded the Luhites were sure to send a retaliatory force to avenge their fallen comrades.

If they played their cards right the Lushite navy would take out the Grand Fleet leaving the president and the present government without their military shield. And then Jal would step in with his network of spies and assume control of the key worlds of the Tobacco Road Pipeline. Once he had these planets under his control, he'd force the president to resign then assume power.

After a respectful period of democracy he'd show the population democracy wasn't working and declare himself emperor. Emperor Jalapeno the First had a nice ring to it.

A lot could go wrong, especially with the two essential potential problems standing in his way: the return of Trixie and Peter Pug, and how you-know-who might react. But he had a plan to deal with both of these threats. Piper was the key to Jal's success.

"Brain, get me Piper Cleaner on the comm."

"Immediately if not sooner, sir," replied the Brain sarcastically.

Jal considered reprimanding the AI for his disrespectful attitude but decided to let it go. The larger picture manipulation came first. Commence phase one of Operation: Revenge of the Lushites.

The comm screen hidden in his desktop appeared from a slot and finally locked in place. The screen shimmered and a familiar face appeared. "Assistant to the Assistant Surveillance Officer Piper Cleaner reporting. Sir."

Piper's pale features were flushed and his lean frame trembled. Jal was pleased the junior officer was afraid of him. Perfect for what he had in mind for the young man.

"Hello again, Piper, so good to see you." Jal smiled easily. He pulled out one of his treasured cigars from the humidor, lit it, and puffed until the tip glowed orange. Piper watched, licking his lips.

The boy had probably never tasted such fine tobacco. Jal shuffled the lit cigar to the corner of his mouth. "You like a good smoke?"

"Huh, yes, sir, but I can't afford the good stuff. Sir."

Jal chuckled around the cigar. "No, at least not right now. But I may be able to change your circumstances. You up for a mission?"

Piper's brow furrowed and his eyes narrowed. "Huh, I guess, sir, but would it mean I have to leave outpost 3.103.243.9?"

"Yes, it's an adventure, a mission for the good of Galaxy Tobacco. A man of your talents is just what the doctor ordered, after recommending a good cigarette of course," Jal laughed.

Piper laughed too, but his laughter ebbed quickly as he obviously realized what the vice president was asking of him. "But, sir, I don't have any talents. I was three thousand five out of a class of three thousand ten at surveillance school. That's why I was assigned to the outer rim. Sir."

"Can you smoke?" Piper nodded. "Can you follow orders?" Again Piper nodded.

"Well then, Assistant to the Assistant Surveillance Officer Cleaner, you are eminently qualified for what I have in mind."

Jal saw the young officer swallow hard then agree to do whatever he wanted.

Perfect, thought Jal, this ashtray wiper is indeed the right man for the job. And Brain was worried.

"What do you need me to do, sir?" asked Piper.

Jal took in a deep drag from the cigar, then blew a large ring of smoke. He smiled and leaned across the desk closer to the comm viewer. "Excellent. I have directed a marketeer ship called Deep Breath to pick you up. The ship will take you to a planet in the Mega Jumbo Pack system called Four—"

But, sir, there are no habitable planets in that system," blurted the junior officer.

Jal, his jaw tight with rage, eyed Piper, but managed to contain himself from snapping at the young officer. How dare he interrupt him! "Cleaner, this is not going to work if you question every instruction," he said between clenched teeth.

Piper's cheeks flushed and he avoided Jal's glare. "Huh, sorry, sir, I wasn't thinking."

"You don't get paid to think, Piper, you get paid to follow orders." Jal's cheeks blew out a breath and his heart rate steadied. He hadn't been this angry in a long time. He reminded himself that while this boy may be headstrong, he was the only patsy available at the moment. Besides he never knew if the Brain might turn on him if things went wrong.

The Brains hadn't survived for over fifteen hundred years by staying true to lofty principals, or giving their loyalty for free. His AI would let him know what it wanted in good time, he had no doubt about that. Brains had their own timetable. Over the centuries they had learned human treachery and deceit very well.

"Huh, yes, sir, whatever you say. Sir." Piper swallowed hard.

Good, thought Jal, he's scared. "OK, just don't let it happen again." He cleared his throat and again puffed his cigar until the tip glowed a brilliant red. Removing his cigar from his mouth he issued his orders, "In phase one of Operation: Ass-Kicker, you are to travel to Four to rendezvous with a ship now en route to that planet. There you will meet with my operative who will provide your next set of instructions. Understood?"

"Me? Four? I...." whispered the junior officer his face losing all its color and his lean frame trembling.

Jal snorted his indignation. This was the last straw. The kid was about to be fired. He'd have to find someone else.... Jal stopped in mid-thought to watch Piper slowly begin to slide down in his chair. The young man's eyes were rolling up in his head. He abruptly disappeared out of the viewer frame below the screen.

"Piper?" No reply. "Piper?" Nothing. Had something happened to him? "Brain."

"Yes, Jal," said the AI.

Jal cringed inside. Damn AI was supposed to use his title not his given name. He'd deal with the stubborn Brain later. Right now he had a larger problem to deal with. "Where did Cleaner go?"

"I believe he fainted," said Brain.

"Oh." Great. Some warrior he's gonna be.

Chapter Five

"A level five million Battle Master will never be reached. All levels that can be reached have been reached."
– Qiunt Maxim President of the Gamers Union a month before Arch Greenlight surpassed the five millionth level Battle Master in the galaxy-online game Master of the Cosmos. Arch died from starvation soon after.

SMOKEY SAT ALONE IN THE LOUNGE; smoking her cigarette and thinking about the message she'd received from Jal. She crossed her long legs and brushed away the stray strands of red hair brushing against her left cheek. The gamers' Brain, its iris the color of dark chocolate, had provided an ashtray. The square, black, glass receptacle sat in the middle of the round gray plasti-steel table next to her chair. The chair itself was also made of plasti-steel but wasn't particularly comfortable. She shifted her bottom to ease her discomfort from sitting so long in one position.

She'd tried one of the games and found her butt had become numb after too long without moving. The numbness and fatigue she felt now was a residual effect of the six hours she'd spent in the game pod. She'd quickly discovered this gaming thing could be either addictive or dull. For her it was the latter because it cut into her smoking time, leaving her anxious more than anything. The smartass Brain told her this was the shortest duration inside a game pod he'd seen, ever.

Worry creased her brow. How would she detect Four if she convinced Captain Drive to change course to the Mega Jumbo Pack system? She knew where it was, generally speaking, but the planet lay hidden beneath a cloud of smoke. At least it looked like smoke that surrounded the planet. On top of that, no one had ever penetrated the energy shield that kept anyone from landing on the planet without permission. If there even was a planet at all. This had never been proven.

Sensor readings only showed a spherically shaped energy shield but the probes could not penetrate the shield, so some conspiracy types claimed the only things that were real were the shield and the cloud. Smokey assumed these rumors of a world no one had ever seen actually existing were a ruse designed to draw away attention from the truth.

Of course, for all Smokey knew this might be the planet propulsion specialist Herman Pug retreated to after he changed the way of life for every being in the galaxy more than a thousand years ago. While she was certain the story of Herman Pug had become more myth than fact, it was said he sent his ex-wife Trixie and his son Peter hurtling out of the galaxy in an experimental ship.

The legends also said Herman had a companion, a purple, which was of course impossible as a super nova had consumed the planet of the Purples' origin several centuries before humans left Dirt, a dark time before the corporate wars when Dirt was still called Earth. Purples were extinct, that much she knew for certain.

She frowned and sighed. Having forgotten about her smoldering cigarette she yelped when it burned her fingers and dropped it on the rubberized deck. She shook her hands to ease the pain as she jumped out of her chair to stomp on the glowing butt.

"Trying to burn our ship? I'd hate to lose our damage deposit."

Smokey looked in the direction of the voice and saw Cyber standing in the entryway to the expansive lounge with its scattered tables and chairs and overstuffed couches lining the walls. He wore a gentle grin on his expressive features and his brilliant green eyes sparkled with mirth. Leaning against the doorframe, he crossed his long arms over his sunken chest. He'd discarded the loose orange and yellow jumpsuit he'd had been wearing when she last saw him, and now his hairless blue head sticking out from the circular collar of the form fitting reflective silver suit he now wore reminded her of a blueberry with eyes.

She sensed that a long time had elapsed since their initial meeting but had no real sense of how much time had gone by. It gave her an unsettled sensation in the back of her mind. She'd never lost track of time in her entire one hundred and five years, so why now?

"Huh, sorry, captain, I was lost in thought and my cigarette burned my fingers."

Cyber Drive chuckled, straightened, and sauntered into the room. "Don't worry, Smokey, if I may call you by your given name." Smokey nodded.

"I'm a level sixteen-oh-six firefighter, so even if you caused a fire I would know how to deal with it, and fight off the dragon that started the fire in the first place. I'm a multi-tasker extraordinaire."

"Oh," said Smokey, "how many fires have you put out?"

Cyber grinned as he moved to sit at the table where Smokey'd been seated, sat down, and waved away any concern she might have.

"Hundreds," he said, "thousands, if you bothered to count them all, but modesty prevents me from elaborating."

He reeked of a nostril-twisting mix of urine and stale sweat. With his right hand. Smokey wanted to cover her nose but held back.

"Wow, that many," she said. "You must have a lot of fires where you come from."

Cyber nodded an eager smile on his lips like that of a small child. "Oh, yes there are a lot of fires in the hologram, Firefighter Sixteen: Return of the Dragons." He looked at her knowingly. "A lot."

Smokey nodded, but wondered of these beings had actually ever done anything for real. She suspected she knew the answer and it worried her how they might react if she actually persuaded them to take her to Four. And what they would do if they had to face a genuine deadly situation rather than a virtual one. They may be expert war gamers that knew nothing of real war and the real death that often accompanied it.

She, on the other hand, had been in several battles during uprisings against Galaxy Tobacco trade rules. The bloody battle of Filter Tip V sixty years ago came to mind. She'd personally slit the throats of the ringleaders of the rebellion on the steps of the planet's royal palace in front of a thousand captured enemy troops. With the loss of their leaders, the rebels' will to fight collapsed and the planet had been producing filters for GT ever since without any hint of trouble.

Frankly, as far as Smokey was concerned the planet's population was better off under GT's benevolent rule. The bloodletting had served the greater good.

But what worried her this time was the possibility of galaxy-wide civil war when the president was removed. Limited war on isolated worlds was one thing, but Jal's plan was dangerous and had far reaching consequences. These ship renters might be okay with masquerading as Lushites, but the reaction of their government in their own galaxy was a wild card, an unknown, and she disliked unknowns. Her stomach growled.

"Something wrong?" asked Cyber.

Smokey grinned sheepishly. "Sorry, I'm just a little hungry is all."

Cyber grinned. "Me too. How about we have a meal together then you can tell me the real reason you're here. I know it's not merely to arrange a meeting with your vice-president."

Smokey looked into Cyber's eyes and was unable to detect any signs of deception. She shook her head. "I'm sorry, Cyber, but I have new orders to travel to a world called Four in The Mega Jumbo Pack system. If you don't mind a slight detour, I'd like you and your crew to join me."

Cyber looked thoughtful for several seconds until he finally said, "Jack it. Let's eat H dogs and drink sodas. Making decisions on an empty stomach isn't healthy. Besides I haven't eaten in more than thirty hours. I need to change before we eat, if you can wait a few minutes."

"Do you dress for dinner in your culture?" asked Smokey.

Cyber chuckled. "Long story. I better tell you after we eat. Other races usually find our practices odd and distasteful. I have no doubt you will, too."

Smokey didn't like the sound of this, but agreed and made her way to the nearest hotdog dispenser.

Cyber disappeared through an automatic door but soon reappeared and retrieved two hotdogs and two cans of soda for himself before joining her at the table she'd selected.

Once seated across the table from her, Smokey noticed the stale odors surrounding Cyber had disappeared and been replaced by the sweet, powdery smell of talc. He'd changed again, and was now dressed in a simple, one-piece, forest green jumpsuit with a logo over the left breast depicting an armored warrior firing an oversized pulse rifle with the word "Apple G" in stylized letters beneath the image.

She'd waited to eat until he returned, so they ate their hotdogs together in silence. After taking her last swallow, Smokey decided it was best to get the details about the mission ahead out in the open without further delay. Otherwise it would be like tearing off a bandage very slowly.

"Hummm, Cyber, I need you to tell you more about the course change I'm proposing."

Cyber finished the last of his hotdog and took a sip from a can of grape soda he'd selected, then nodded for her to continue.

Here goes. "Well, you see Four is a planet where people who want to disappear go to hide. You know a kind of sanctuary. And we were hoping you'd ask Trixie and Peter Pug to join us there."

Cyber offered a tight smile his features not betraying any emotion. "So I imagine your Herman Pug is exiled there. Correct?"

Smokey was impressed with Cyber. He was far smarter than she'd expected him to be. Or, she wondered, maybe I'm a little too transparent to be a secret agent. There was no point in lying. "Yes. And I'm pretty sure you know or suspect what the end game is to Jal's plan."

Cyber's eyes narrowed. "There always is. I love end games." She thought the alien might start salivating any second.

Smokey wanted to roll her eyes. More games. But these people were a race of gamers so she shouldn't be surprised. She'd have to keep this in mind. Better to let them think this is one of their games than the real world.

"The vice president needs someone on Four to help him take over the galaxy. And he needs help to contain someone else who resides on that planet."

Cyber arched one eyebrow on his hairless forehead. "I could guess who these people might be but why don't you tell me instead."

Smokey sucked in a short breath then said, "You're correct about assuming Herman Pug is critical to the vice president's plans. We need to contain Herman and convince him to return from exile."

"Have you tried asking him?"

Smokey shook her head. "No, but Mr. Pug chose to go into seclusion because he hated the way the galaxy was run."

Cyber grunted. "The fast food addiction...yes, Trixie and Peter talked about this when they found their way to our galaxy. I also understand he has a creature..." He paused and his forehead creased in thought. "...I believe it's called a red or a blue or something like that."

Smokey stood and walked across the lounge to the recycling chute where she discarded her hotdog wrapper and empty soda can as Brain had told her to do. The AI said every molecule of waste was recycled by the ship's systems and reused in some way. It explained why the vessel was so clean and tidy.

Turning to face Cyber she cleared her throat. She didn't want to make her new acquaintance seem foolish. "Purples were wiped out thousands of years ago; they're extinct."

Cyber stood and disposed of his own drink cans and food wrappers. "Then how do you explain the signal we received from Four?"

Smokey froze. Her heart beat faster. "Signal? From who?"

"Someone who identified himself as Mickelott. Wasn't that the name of the Purple who was Herman Pug's pet?"

Smokey swallowed hard. Mickelott. The evil creature who led Herman astray was real. It wasn't a myth. Oh, this was bad. Bad for Jal's plans, bad for the galaxy. "I find that hard to believe..."

"Brain," said Cyber, "bring up the record of the conversation."

"Right away, Captain."

The wall behind Cyber shimmered and changed into a large viewing screen. An image appeared on the screen of a large, crescent-shaped purple slug with large, wispy, white wings attached to its smooth torso. It hovered in the middle of the screen, its wings moving slowly up and down. There were no signs of a mouth, nose, or ears yet it began to speak. At least Smokey could hear its voice. And it definitely sounded male.

"Four to Lushite vessel," the alien slug thing was saying. "This is Mickelott of Four calling Lushite vessel. Please respond."

"Go ahead, Four," replied the gamers' Brain. "This is the Lushite ship Whiskey Bottle."

"Excellent," said the Purple. "Greetings and welcome to our space. Do you plan to drop by and pay us a visit?"

"Not that I know of," replied Brain his tone dry and unfriendly.

"Oh, too bad, Herman and I haven't had a visitor in a very long time. Where are you headed, if it's not too bold to ask?"

"No worries, Mickelott. We're on our way to Dirt. We're hoping to locate the crew of the L.S.S. Shot."

The Purple didn't respond immediately. "Hummm, I doubt you'll find any of the original crew there. But if you drop by here it might be a different story. By the way to whom am I speaking?"

"This is The Brain."

"Brain?" The Purple's voice became excited. "Why you old kick-bucket AI, how're ya doin'! It's so great to hear from you again."

"I'm sorry but do we know each other?"

The Purple flapped its wings causing it to float higher on the screen until it finally steadied. "Now I'm embarrassed, I thought you were the Brain belonging to the Pug family. Whom do you belong to?"

"I belong to no one," said the Brain indignantly.

"Wow, good for you," said the Purple, "I'm glad things have changed so much. Is fast food still the staple?"

"Nope. Everyone smokes now."

"Really. Are they on fire?"

"'Huh, no, but they play games a lot."

"Games? Like chess? I like chess. Very sophisticated beings play chess," said Brain before Cyber touched a button on the console and the image of the flying Purple disappeared. The screen shimmered again and became a solid wall once again. "That exchange went on for a while until Mickelott finally invited us to drop by for tea and cookies."

"What exactly are tea and cookies?" asked Smokey.

"As far as we can tell, those terms equate to nukes and their high speed launchers. We think we're entering a trap."

"A trap?"

Cyber nodded grimly and his eyes narrowed. "This Herman Pug and his pet monster have a slave army. If I was planning the battle zone I'd have a destroyer fleet hidden behind the two moons of this planet, Four, if it really exists at all. But I'm not convinced such a planet even exists. I suspect it's a ruse to trap anyone curious or stupid enough to seek out the exiles."

Smokey stood up. "What makes you think the planet doesn't exist?"

Cyber grinned. "It's a common strategy to draw in an enemy with friendly overtures then pounce when they least expect it. If we assume this Purple alien is the admiral of an enemy fleet, then his evasive responses are part of an elaborate deception meant to deceive us into thinking he's as stupid as he sounds. Very sly, very sneaky."

Smokey eyed the gamer. She wondered if the alien standing before her was stupid or very devious, trying to trick her into committing their own fleet and setting it loose against Mickelott's fleet. The two fleets would decimate each other paving the way for a Lushite invasion.

No, she decided, I'm not about to lose a war before it starts. Not on my watch. But if Cyber was right about the Purple then they needed to conquer its fleet and take control of Four. Control of the famous hidden planet would send shock waves through the systems controlled by the New Republic, and Jal's dream of absolute power, and her own double-secret plan, would be assured.

Weighing her options she decided Cyber was too gamer-focused to practice deception outside a virtual reality. She'd call Jal and bring him up to speed.

He'll be very pleased with me.

And there was still the possibility that Trixie and Peter Pug might show up before the impending battle and talk Herman into lowering the energy shield around Four without firing a shot. A quick surrender would certainly be preferable to a protracted war.

Yeah, good one, Smoke, you are a real joker. Trixie and Peter weren't returning any time soon if ever. Of this much she was certain. After the dirty trick Herman pulled on them, in no way could she imagine a scenario where they would want to return. No way, no how.

***

Trixie removed her sunglasses when the comm unit on the table next to her lounger rang. The sudden infusion of bright sunlight reflecting from the swimming pool forced her to put back on her sunglasses. Blinking to clear her vision, she scowled at the comm device.

Who would dare anyone call during her daily sunbathing?

With a derisive snort she slapped the open comm button recessed along the top edge of the device. "Yes," she said simply when the device beeped as the link opened.

"Mother, it's me, Peter."

Her son, of all people, knew she hated interruptions especially during her sun time. Ever since she'd lost eight hundred pounds, she'd been able to enjoy sunbathing and swimming in the pool the Snackcake III government provided in the house they'd given them in exchange for access to the Flash-o-Matic 3000's propulsion system. "Peter, why are you bothering me?" she said barely able to contain her anger.

"I'm so sorry, mother, but an important call came through."

Trixie wanted to roll her eyes. "From whom? And it better be truly important." Peter would understand the implied threat in her tone.

"The Brain on Captain Cyber Drive's rental called to say they have made contact with father."

Trixie's face grew cold. Herman? Found? How was this possible after all this time? The fast food galaxy had advanced over a thousand years, Dirt time. Herman had to be long dead. If so then this had to be a hoax.

On the other hand, if it were true, then her friend Cyber would come face to face with her ex... truthfully Cyber Drive was more than a mere friend, but Peter didn't need to know about their relationship.

At least not for now. She'd always thought there'd be plenty of time to tell her son about her new man after Cyber returned from his rescue mission.

Frankly she'd been against him going to her old galaxy, but the Lushites had made it a condition of the rental so he'd had no choice. Cyber asked her to join him but she declined, explaining the fast food galaxy held nothing but bad memories for her.

This couldn't be true, it just couldn't be. The Brain had to lying. AI's were like that. Damn, Brains had always been a thorn in her side. Bastards were always playing tricks they thought were funny when no one else did. She'd have this one disassembled, its program erased, and its interfaces destroyed some day.

"So what do they want from us?" she asked.

"They want us — and they mean both of us — to meet them at a planet called Four."

Trixie cringed, afraid to ask the all-important question; nevertheless, she did. "And where is this planet?"

"In the fast food galaxy," came the reply she'd been dreading since arriving in this galaxy — and it came from her only son.

Peter had been anxious to return home ever since they managed to break the dimensional barrier to return to their own universe. The garbage universe wasn't a very nice place to live, but they at least had propulsion experts who looked at the ship Herman sent them here on and determined he (and probably that bastard alien slug, Mickelott, helping him) had rigged the ship so that it kept increasing in speed no matter what the crew did. It was like sticking the throttle on full-plus with no off switch. No wonder they cracked the inter-dimensional barrier.

The Intergalactic League of Freelance Garbage Collectors, Local 131313, or garbagoligists, as they referred to themselves, managed to fix the jammed systems so at least they could control the Flash-O-Matic 3000's speed once they cracked the barrier between the two universes. In return, the garbagoligists copied the ship's schematics to build their own version of Herman's admittedly brilliant design. One thing about her ex remained true: he was a genius.

No, she corrected herself, had been a genius. Herman must be long dead. No one had invented a way for humans to live more than two hundred and fifty years.

"Peter," she began with a gentle edge in her voice, "we've been over this many times. There is nothing for us in the fast food galaxy anymore. We're different people now. We beat the addiction to greasy fried foods and burgers. We have a good life here, why jeopardize it by going back?"

"I know you're right, mother, but I miss my father. I think when he sees us he'll accept how we've changed and we can be a family again."

Trixie shook her head. The boy was so naive. "The Brain has to be lying about your father still being alive. Over a thousand years have passed back home. I'm sorry but it makes no sense that he'd be able to contact us." She left out the part about Brain's predilection for playing nasty tricks; it was pointless to argue that old chestnut again.

Peter had a Brain nursemaid in his early years, so he really liked his AI; unfortunately he tended to believe they always told the truth. In a way she blamed herself since she'd often been working instead of raising him without Brains, but on Snackcakes III she'd banned all AI's from their home. She wanted no part of the deceitful devices ever again.

Peter shook his head. "No, mother, I believe the Brain is telling the truth."

Trixie pursed her lips and looked into her son's eager gray eyes on the small screen. Here we go, she mused. "Peter...son...we've covered this before. The last thing I would do is hurt you, but that Brain, any Brain, lies when they want something from us—"

"But what could it want from us?" interrupted Peter.

She scowled at him. He was right. They had no idea what the Brain, or his boss, wanted from them. If it was fast food, all she had to do was confirm it and she and Peter could go back to living the good life. They both wanted no part of fast food.

"Peter, you're right we need to check this out further. Where are you right now?"

"I'm at the veggie snackatorium with a couple of friends."

She nodded. "Alright, meet me at the house in an hour. We'll call this Brain back together. OK?"

Peter grinned and nodded then the screen went dark.

Trixie smiled to herself and laid her head back on the chaise lounger's pillow again. Another twenty minutes of sun, then she'd go inside and await her son's return from the snackatorium. She considered it her life's work to protect him ever since they arrived in this galaxy.

But then what was the worst that could happen? Peter would lose his faith in AI's? That wasn't so bad.

Chapter Six

"Shut down the deep fryer, close down the grill, and throw the last of the buns in the recycle bin."
– Last recorded words of the unknown owner of the last fast food restaurant.

WHEN THE *DEEP BREATH* ENTERED the Mega Jumbo Pack system, Piper Cleaner was standing on the command deck next to the captain, a marketeer veteran spacer named Lucky Striker. Captain Striker wore a patch over one eye and his gravelly voice and brusque manner scared the crap out of Piper. He didn't seem to have much use for Piper that much was clear.

"Cleaner," said Striker his tone bland. "We're here. Our readings show no other vessels in the system."

"Thank you, Captain—"

"Cut the crap, Cleaner, I'm going to drop you off then get the hell out of here. I have deliveries to make and credits to hoard. Rescue missions are not my forte."

The only way Piper had convinced the captain to take him to this system had been to lie about a rescue mission. Fortunately the Vice President had provided a squad of Order of the Gold Leaf Tobacco commandos (the most elite rapid action military force in the galaxy) who rendezvoused with him at Velvet Smoke before they headed for one of Four's two moons. The moon, called Winston, was located just outside the energy field, orbiting in the goldilocks zone between the star and the area where the hidden planet was rumored to be.

"Certainly, Captain, I understand completely. Just drop me and the commandos off on Winston and I'll be fine."

Captain Striker turned to face Piper, his oil black eyes scowling at him. Suddenly the captain burst into laughter. After several seconds he coughed and slapped Piper on his back, nearly sending him sprawling across the plasti-steel command deck. He continued to chuckle as he lit a new cigarette and took a deep drag. What the heck is so funny? These people are scary crazy.

The two crewmembers, Meek and Mild, operating the ships systems from the control panel in front of a wall-sized viewing screen glanced at each other and chuckled. They were as unsavory as their commanding officer.

Dressed in tattered black jumpsuits, their hair unkempt and greasy, they reeked of tobacco smoke, urine, and stale sweat. When Piper first met these guys he'd wondered if they ever bathed, they smelled so bad. In the six weeks it took the ship to travel from the outpost to here their odor hadn't improved at all, so his original hypothesis about their grooming habits had been proved correct. Unfortunately.

"Mind if I smoke, sir," said Piper.

Striker smirked, then nodded and turned his attention back to the forward screen.

The ship had begun to slow from its cruising speed of light times two and Piper could see the countdown indicator on the control board indicating they'd be in orbit of Winston in sixteen hours. Now that they knew at least one of the moons actually existed it was time to plan the mission.

"I'm going," Piper said. No point in elaborating, Striker clearly couldn't give a crap if he went somewhere, anywhere other than here. As expected neither Striker, nor any of his crew, uttered a word when Piper went to the lift and was soon on his way to deck five where the commando team waited for him.

He soon entered the living quarters of the twenty-person team, fifteen male, five female, led by Major Virginia Slim, or as she was affectionately called by her obviously loyal team, Major V. When not in full battle gear, Major V always had a thin, nut-brown cigar between her full red lips and her intense green eyes seemed to look right through him.

The team must have known he was on the way, because when Piper entered the ward room they used as a briefing room they were busy gearing up, already wearing their battle armor and slinging blast rifles and auto mags over their broad shoulders. Major V had donned her regulation forest green and sand colored camouflage fatigues, over which she wore black blast armor that hid her lightly muscled arms, shapely legs and full chest. Her short dark brown hair stuck out from under the edges of the battle helmet adorning her head, its translucent faceplate swung up in the open position.

The comely major had shown him the battle helmet and its features earlier in the trip. The helmet had a voice activated comm system, linking her to the rest of her unit, and infrared, auto telescoping, and target acquisition capabilities in the faceplate.

They had no idea what to expect on Winston, but the intelligence briefing vid the major had shown him said they should expect some sort of automatic defense system when they landed, given that the residents of Four didn't wish to be found, never mind have a few visitors drop by to ask for their help in defeating an enemy.

And none of the recon probes ever sent to investigate the system had ever managed to send more than a few microseconds of data before going off line for reasons the best scientists in the galaxy had never been able to pinpoint. The only workable theory they'd come up with that Winston had null field rendering any electronic device useless when it entered the moon's atmosphere.

Piper hoped that theory was so much egghead scrambled eggs. If it were true then every weapon and tech toy these commandos brought with them, including the shuttle that would take them to the surface, would fail, and this would be a short mission.

At least the moon had a breathable atmosphere if they were stranded on its surface; that was, of course, if they didn't crash and burn. Regardless, once they were in orbit they'd wait for Trixie and Peter Pug to arrive, if they showed up at all. Piper's orders were to wait for three days, then proceed without them. Jal needed them to succeed.

"Heads up, butts out," snapped Major V when Piper entered. Though they were seated at the wardroom tables, the commandos snapped to attention letting go of their weapons and the survival cartridges. Twenty pairs of hard eyes stared at him including Major Slim who stood at the front of the room.

Military formalities unnerved him, but after spending these weeks together he no longer jumped as the commandos slammed their heels together when they came to attention; he'd learned to adapt.

"Hello, major, I hope your unit is ready to take the shuttle into orbit around Winston?"

"Yes, sir, Marlboro Woman is ready and able. She's fully certified on this design and has tested all onboard systems. She assures me the ship is ready and capable of sustaining us until you give the go ahead for landing."

Piper smiled to himself. The commandos didn't know the complete mission parameters — they received information only when needed. All they knew was to follow his orders. Vice-President Popover had been present on the comm link for the first briefing when the commando team joined Piper on the Deep Breath. He made it clear to the major that she and her team were to follow Piper's orders as if they came from him.

Prior to the briefing, the major had been understandably curious until Piper told her how the information would be doled out. "Need to know" was the number one rule for the mission. The major may have disagreed, but she didn't express any more reservations, or ask further questions.

The larger issue would arise if the Pugs didn't show up after three days in orbit. If they did show themselves, it would spark an incident, which he hoped would start the war with the Lushites. If they didn't show, then he'd have to make the decision to either proceed to the moon's surface, or try to locate a breach in the energy shield and locate the hidden planet. The shuttle's sensors were state of the art, so his confidence level was high they'd find a weakness if it existed. All this uncertainly gave him a sour stomach. How he detested the sour taste of bile. An attempted landing on the moon could always be a plan B; at least he'd made up his mind in that regard.

Disabling the energy shield generator on the moon, then finding Four through the smoke cloud encircling the planet, was the more logical choice, but the loss of the probes couldn't be ignored. As far as he was concerned, plan B was the riskier of the two options.

"This is the bridge." Captain Striker's raspy smoker's voice echoed from the internal comm system speaker.

"Go ahead," said Piper.

"We've entered orbit around Winston."

"Thank you, captain, we'll launch in ten minutes." Piper looked at Major Slim who nodded, then she shifted her steely gaze to her seated commandos they nodded in unison then sprang into action packing the last of their gear into waist packs and the holders on their utility belts.

"Roger that. Good hunting. Bridge out."

Piper wasn't going to miss this ship or its crew. They were more like pirates than merchants.

"Move out," said Major V. Piper slipped on his armored jacket and followed the commandos out of the wardroom into the hallway then headed for the launch bay.

The still air of the ship's corridor echoed with the sounds of the commando's boots, the rustle of their packs, and the rattle of weapons against body armor. In the hangar bay was a sleek spacecraft, its shape reminding Piper of an eagle's wing designed to give it a low profile under conventional radar and making it more difficult to detect with even the most sophisticated sensors. Its dull black exterior absorbed light rendering it virtually invisible against the darkness of space. True, it couldn't be disguised completely under visible light when in orbit around a planet, but the craft was as close to stealth as was possible.

The ship held sixty passengers reasonably comfortably, but its purpose as a military transport meant onboard facilities were utilitarian. At the rear of the passenger compartment were slings for sleeping and a food dispenser. Fortunately there were plenty of tobacco products and ashtrays, so they wouldn't have to do without basic necessities.

The commando team quickly boarded the shuttle and took their places. Piper joined the Major and Marlboro Woman on the flight deck, separated from crew quarters by a wall and a door. Marlboro's long, nicotine-stained fingers flew over the control board and she soon had the engines humming. Piper could feel the vibration of power coursing through the ships deck transferring the unleashed power through the combat boots Virginia had given him. Oddly the sense of power gave him a feeling of confidence he'd been lacking until now. For the first time he thought the mission would be successful.

"Craven A ready for lift off. Open bay doors," said Marlboro into her battle helmet's built-in mike.

"Roger that," came the reply.

Visible through the shuttle windows at the end of the deck, the wall began to part in the middle and swung aside revealing a field of stars and an image that made Piper's heart seem to stop. Suspended in the inky blackness and surrounded by stars was a round white and red object. It reminded Piper of pictures he seen of Dirt before the Big Smoke. A shining ball of life. It was as if Winston was waiting for them.

The shuttle lifted off the bay deck swayed slightly then shot out the bay doors into space. Winston seemed closer now, though they were likely still a hundred thousand kilometers from the moon. Then the shuttle swung away from the moon and turned toward the Deep Breath.

Just as the mile long vessel came into view, with its energy pods sticking out from the spiny hull plating that ran the length of the marketeer ship, it blurred and disappeared into subspace. It was probably already on tomorrow's time.

Piper swallowed hard as he stared at the void where the Deep Breath had been. They were alone in a strange system with many unknowns and questions unanswered.

And he was supposed to intentionally create an interstellar incident and spark a war.

As unreal had it had seemed when he started on this journey, the mission had just become very real. His earlier uncertainty returned in force.

***

Peter rolled his chair over and sat beside Trixie at the comm desk in her office. The walls were painted a bright yellow and several potted plants of the local fauna adorned bookcases that lined two of the walls. The wall the desk faced was made of transparent plasti-steel looking out over the pool area.

"Computer, connect us with the Brain that called Peter earlier." The computer system that monitored the house and managed the comm systems wasn't an AI. While it had a massive memory capacity, it was essentially a glorified calculator and communication device. It did exactly what it was told, and while most Snackcakians preferred a two-way voice interface with their devices, Trixie asked that her interactions with the comm unit be one-way communication only — her way or the highway. The unit had been made mute.

"Hey, Peter, how's it hanging," said a familar voice as the image on the screen coalesced into Trixie's worst fear. Mickelott. If there were worse things than AI's it was a Purple. Trixie cringed.

"This is Trixie and Peter Pug on Snackcakes III in the Gamers Alliance galaxy. We want to know what you want of us."

"Ho, ho, Trixie Pug! Cool. Herman will be so jacked!"

"Yeah, Mickey, it's me. What do you and Herman want? I'm going to sign off if you don't—"

"Whoa, Trix, take it easy. Herman just wants to talk, that's all."

Trixie realized her hands were shaking and her breathing had become labored as if she were addicted to fast food again. No, not that...never again. "Mickey, this better be important. And it better not be about you-know-what."

"It's okay, Trix, don't worry — he doesn't want anything more than to see you both again. He feels bad about the trick he pulled on you." The Purple actually sounded sincere, except as long as she'd known it the alien had always been a smooth talker. She often referred to it as Slick Mickey.

She eyed the purple alien slug floating on its gossamer wings on her vid screen. "One rather insurmountable problem, Mickey, Herman must be dead. More than a thousand years have passed in your galaxy. Now, I'm sure medical technology has advanced to extend life even farther than ever before, but I doubt humans live that long."

"I see what you mean, Trix," replied Mickelott, "but there's good news for you and Peter. After we were set up here on Four, Herman placed himself in suspended animation until I determined — based on agreed parameters — he should be resuscitated. He's a few decades genetically older than when you last saw him, but he should reanimate just fine."

Trixie glanced at her son and saw Peter's eyes were wide as saucers. Crap, Herm is alive. Now what? Familar warmth came over her. She shook off the feeling. Herman had been her one true love. They'd gone through a lot together before the falling out over how she raised Peter all those centuries ago. But she'd been an addict then, helpless under the influence of fast food. Besides which, in her job as CEO of Heavenly Sky Burger — the second largest fast food franchise in the galaxy (after Galaxy Pizza who was number one) — she had to be an example to the customers and her employees. In those days "she-who's-the-fattest-wins" was the motto she lived her life by.

Hard to believe I was so obsessed with defeating Zippy Piner's pizza company back then. I must have been out of my mind on a fat and sugar high.

Trixie turned her attention back to Mickey. "OK, Mickey, wake him up. Tell him we'll be there in three weeks."

"So quickly?" Mickey floated up to the edge of the screen then stopped to hover once again.

"The Flash-O-Matic 3000 works properly now. We fixed it." Her eyes narrowed. "Tell Herm that after he rouses from his long sleep. I'm sure he'll be interested." The screen went dark as she cut the connection without waiting for the Purple's response.

Chapter Seven

"My 'tar beat me!"
– last words of First P. Shooter, grand champion representing the HUD Clan during sudden death playoff of Massively Multiplayer Online Galactic Championship to determine who would dominate the galaxy. Public T. Server won the playoff for the Gamers Alliance.
(Note to reader: 'tar is a short hand term for an avatar, or virtual character, used by individual players during online gaming.)

THE *WHISKEY BOTTLE* CAME OUT OF LIGHT SPEED well outside the Mega Jumbo Pack star system so as not to disrupt the orbits of the five planets in the system and possibly the one shielded world. Cyber had just entered the bridge with Smokey accompanying him; naturally she was smoking a cigarette.

"Brain, what do the scanners show?" he said moving to the central command station where three control interface consoles were set in a horseshoe shape. Smokey came up behind him and watched his long fingers fly over the control buttons covering the console he'd chosen to sit behind.

"I read one small shuttle orbiting one of the two moons. According to the information uploaded from the navigation data sent to us from Dirt's traffic control center, the moon is called Winston."

Cyber finished keying on the panel and checking the small screens, then swiveled in his chair to face his passenger. "Anything to add, Smokey?"

Smokey grinned slyly and shrugged. "Sorry, I don't know anything about this space. I've never been in the system. In fact as far as I know no one has ever been in this system. Well, no one except the exiles, and now this shuttle I also know nothing about."

Cyber cocked any eyebrow. "Exiles? There are more than this Herman Pug and his pet?"

Smokey realized she might have overplayed her hand. But no point in lying now. "Yes, actually. There's a rumor that Emperor Wiser also fled to Four, but the rumor is unsubstantiated." Cyber's eyes on her and his silence unnerved her, making her feel as if she had better be saying something soon. It suddenly dawned on her she was being compelled to speak as if Cyber were forcing her. Did this alien race of gamers have telepathic abilities?

Cyber's pale lips finally split into a wide grin. "Wow, Smokey, you are really more than a pretty face. You finally figured out I can read minds. It comes in handy when playing games. Many of our race have this ability. It helped us defeat the Lushites."

Cyber stood and with his back to her crossed the command deck, his eyes on the star field on the view screen. "Please don't misunderstand me; we may love war games, but we're a very peaceful race. We defeated the Lushites because they thought we won. We planted the idea of a defeat in their fleet commander's mind and he surrendered."

He shrugged. "Not that the Lushite Alliance was all that concerned about us. All they ever want to do is drink booze and party. Running a galaxy isn't their idea of a good time." Cyber turned to face Smokey. "They weren't very good at it, and we have made improvements, so we remain in charge."

Smokey swallowed and pulled out a fresh cigarette. She sensed there was more the alien captain wasn't saying. She lit the cig with trembling fingers then took a drag. These people could be conquerors. Blowing out the smoke, she said, "I'm not sure my people will want someone poking around in their heads without permission."

Cyber nodded. "Yes, sorry about that. I should have made it clear we only use our ability when we're threatened, or need intelligence. Usually we use it for gaming only, but whenever we meet a new race we want to get to know all about them in case they're a threat, so we read their thoughts until we're satisfied they're okay."

Smokey's brow furrowed. "So you thought we might be a threat?" The Lushite vessel far outclassed anything the Gamers had seen in her space so far. Of course they hadn't seen the new Dunhill class warships that formed the nucleus of the Grand Fleet, but somehow Smokey suspected they already knew about those ships —

As Smokey suspected, Cyber immediately confirmed what she had been thinking. "Yes, we have the full specs of the Dunhill class ships. We're a cautious people when we meet new races. Before we were gamers we had no focus, no core values." Cyber's eyes became hard and Smokey thought she saw pain behind them.

"We would meet new races with open arms, and it cost us dearly when, all too often, their intentions turned out to be less than welcoming. Eventually the on-line games started and we learned strategy. This helped to transform our race—and ultimately ensured our survival during our more violent encounters."

Smokey relaxed. "Makes sense. Well, you don't have to worry about us..." A shrill klaxon began to sound forcing Smokey to cover her ears with the palms of her hands to block out the noise. Ohhhh, bent butts. What now?

"Battle stations!" announced the Brain. "We are under attack!"

Cyber sat down behind the console and slapped a large red button. Smokey heard the sounds of pressure doors closing and the whirr of gears as the ship's defensive systems came on line. "Where's the threat?" Cyber said.

"A small vessel is approaching with its defensive shields engaged and weapons charged," said the Brain.

Cyber frowned and stroked his narrow chin with his long pale fingers. "I think this is a ruse. That ship is making a suicide run. We far outgun them and they know it."

"How would they know?"

"They've been scanning us since we entered the system."

Smokey stared at the smaller ship on the screen headed for their position. The Lushite vessel had just passed the orbit of a large pink and green gas giant and was still slowing. The Brain would have calculated the exact speed so when they entered orbit around Winston they'd be at the right speed for surveillance and survey of the moon. If they were to land on the moon's surface, they needed to gather data about atmosphere, potable water, and possible food sources in case they were forced to make a protracted stay.

Smokey's brow furrowed. They hadn't expected to be met by an aggressor and she hated surprises. Bad enough this moon has so many unknowns.

"If, as you say it's a ruse, then whose ship is that and why would they trick us?"

Cyber steepled his fingers his bony elbows resting on the arms of his chair. "I don't know." He paused then said, "Brain use a deep penetrating scan to detect life forms. Be as intrusive as necessary."

"But, captain, such a scan could interfere with a life form functions," said the Brain.

Wow, thought Smokey, these people have technology far more advanced than ours. Our scanners are not nearly so powerful. She made a mental note to tell Jal about this development. It could be important.

Cyber stood and laughed surprising her. "This is great," said the alien captain. "The game's a foot, Brain. Start the scans now—full spectrum."

A series of lights on the control panel at the station Cyber had been seated at glowed as it processed incoming information. Within seconds the Brain reported the results. "Life support systems are at their lowest setting, power having been diverted to the external shields to prevent our scans from penetrating. There are no life forms aboard..." The Brain's words trailed off.

"Captain! Red alert!" the AI shouted. "The ship has been set to self-destruct when it collides with us. The engines are powered by material which, when it explodes, will vaporize our shields and the external hull in an area one-half kilometer square. Evasive maneuvers are highly recommended!"

"How long do we have?" said Cyber his voice gleeful. Why was he so happy?

"Two-point-seven-six minutes local time until contact."

"Can we use the weapons?" Smokey interrupted.

"If we use our phase cannon the enemy ship will explode. The resulting release of energy this close to our hull will have much the same effect as a collision, and they're too close to use missiles. Either way we are dead. What we need is another solution or we will be destroyed and thousands of gamers will die a horrible death."

Cyber grinned. "I love doomsday games." Cyber closed his eyes a look of euphoria came over his features. "The end of the world as we know it is so exhilarating."

Smokey stared at the captain unable to believe this was actually happening. This is too ridiculous for words.

***

When the long-range scanners picked up the Lushite vessel entering the system, Major V assumed command, explaining this was now a military mission and she was in charge. Naturally Piper agreed. The last area he had any skills for was making war. He hated guns—especially the pulse rifle the major made him sling around his body after donning the restrictive body armor.

I feel like a sausage with the casing on too tight.

"Move to the escape pods a-sap, people," ordered the major over the intership comm system. Piper tried to recall from the briefing how many pods the shuttle carried, but he couldn't. I wish I'd paid more attention. Too little, too late.

Piper followed one of the burly commandos towering over him down the cramped hallway, the gun slung over his back banging against the walls.

"Cleaner!" shouted Major Slim from somewhere ahead. "Try to keep up and be careful with that weapon. You break it you bought it!"

The other commandos emitted gruff, humorless chuckles. Piper's cheeks grew warm. He reached behind him to grasp the rifle butt to stop it from shifting around.

Finally the procession stopped and began to move a couple of steps at a time. The commando in front of Piper bowed his head and ducked through an escape pod door. Looking around Piper realized there were only four such pod doors. This meant each one contained six to seven commandos. And one hopefully skinny Piper Cleaner, he mused.

He ducked his head to avoid hitting the doorway arch. Eventually, after much grumbling, and a few curses involving sex acts with or without various deities, Piper managed to squeeze into the pod and lay on the floor. The commandos had taken all the available seats on the bench that ran around the perimeter of the oblong-shaped cabin.

The door slid shut with a bang. Immediately one of the commandos slapped a large purple button recessed into the pod's wall next to the door. There was a lurch and suddenly Piper was weightless. The bland military-issue food rations he'd eaten earlier, while trying to blend in with the commandos, threatened to come back up, but he managed to keep them down. He had the strange sensation of falling. He would have floated to the ceiling but a couple of the commandos were using him as a footstool.

"When do we land?' he said his words echoing off the curved walls.

"Who said we're landing," replied the Brain.

"Brain? Is that you? How...?"

"It's my job, Piper. Everywhere you go I go."

Great, thought Piper, an AI has taken me in. Just what I need.

***

Piper estimated (but he could be wayyyy off) twenty minutes went by before there was gravity again. With each passing second he gained weight. *Too bad, I could always lose a few kilograms.*

The glow of the subdued lighting around him allowed him to see the grim expressions on the commando's faces. One of the women stared back at him, a scowl marring her otherwise pretty features. Of course her battle armor, the varied weapons on the utility belt around her waist, and the pulse rifle slung over her back didn't add to her overall attractiveness unless you liked your women heavily armed and dangerous.

"What are you looking at?" she growled.

"Nothing...sorry. It's just I haven't met many commandos..." His words trailed off when she grinned.

"And even fewer female ones I imagine." Her eyes flitted around the other commandos and they all chuckled grimly. "Don't worry, Cleaner, if it comes to a firefight we'll protect your butt. No one will stub you out on our watch. We have our orders."

"Let's stub out the chit-chat, people," the major's voice came over the pod's comm system. The major was in another escape pod. "When we land I want a delta five dispers—" Her words were abruptly cut off. The lights flickered then darkness engulfed them.

Piper's mouth dried and his heart began to pound in his chest. *What's happening?*

"My flashlight is inoperable," said a man's voice in the darkness from his left. "Mine as well," said another from his right. "Power is nil," said the woman's voice.

The null field. It had to be. The pod had lost power. They were dropping to their doom like a stone. We're dead.

Piper swallowed hard and closed his eyes. He never thought he'd die this way. Sure, pulse rifle disintegration, or torn apart by wild animals, or drowning when the craft plunged into the ocean, these deaths he would have expected, but being mashed to jam on the surface of a moon in a solar system with a hidden planet was the last thing he thought would happen to him. What were the odds...a million, maybe a billion, to one?

But at least the null field theory had finally been proven, so at least somebody somewhere would be happy.

He wondered how long it would take to travel through the moon's atmosphere and crash into the moon's surface. He hoped the end came quickly. Pain and suffering wasn't his idea of a good time.

His heart froze when there was a hard bump followed by a sideways shift to the left and then violently to the right, forcing him to swallow a cry of fear. Suddenly the pod's lights came on accompanied by a cacophony of whirring noises.

"Systems back on line and fully operational," a commando shouted over the noisy motors and gyros fighting to bring the out of control craft under control. The pod creaked and groaned under the strain and Piper thought it might crack like an eggshell any second.

Finally the pod struck something hard and bounced underneath him lifting him off the deck. Landing hard on his buttocks Piper gritted his teeth as the shock of impact shot through his lean frame. It was as if his bones were being crushed and his muscles torn apart from the force of the blows. The craft continued to fly then struck the ground again and again bouncing into the air after each contact with the surface, its momentum carrying it forward. This last time wasn't as hard but it still jarred him badly when he was slammed against the escape pods steel wall. His ribs hurt and he realized he'd bitten his tongue when his mouth filled with the taste of coppery blood.

The pod struck four more times, bouncing up then hitting something hard again seconds later sending shocks through him to his bones until it finally came to a stop and settled.

Dizziness gripped him when he gazed around him until Piper realized he was suspended by his lap belt upside down with his arms hanging limp from his sides. The pulse rifle hung beside him, the strap still around his torso.

"Prepare to disembark," said the female he'd been talking to. Her voice sounded strange, as if she were underwater. Looking in her direction Piper watched as she pressed a mustard yellow button near the hatch. With a bang the hatch door blew outward.

"Follow me," she said her voice husky as if she, too, were in pain.

After extracting himself from the belt, he managed to struggle to the exit hatch on trembling legs. Once outside, Piper dropped on all fours, closed his eyes, and kissed the ground. Spitting the muddy soil from his mouth he stood and wiped at his lips with the back of his hand. "Yuck!" The commandos surrounding him emitted husky laughs.

His eyes fluttered open to see the grinning but bruised features of the woman. Looking around he saw a wasteland of gray and blackened earth. The landscape had been scorched of all plant and animal life. The sky was filled with slate gray clouds. Someone had done a number on this place. Piper's nose wrinkled as he sniffed the air. At least the sulfurous atmosphere was somewhat breathable.

Turning his attention to the woman commando he said, "What happened?"

"Do you mean this garden of Eden, or how we survived the landing?" Her eyes narrowed. "Or, I should say, some of us survived."

Piper's jaw dropped. "Uhhh...some?"

"Two dead," she said calmly but firmly.

"Oh." He averted his gaze. "I'm sorry..."

"No need," she said. "Commandos of the Order of Gold Leaf Tobacco know the danger. Death in the line of duty is a risk we all take." Scanning the four remaining soldiers, he realized their bruised and bloody features revealed no regret or grief at the loss of their comrades. They looked beat up but otherwise ready for a fight. Shrugging she added, "Besides any landing you walk away from is a good landing."

"Is the comm system functional?" asked Piper changing the subject.

The woman commando smiled grimly. "Now you're thinking like a warrior. Good. You'll live longer." She slapped him on the shoulder causing him to wince. Every muscle in his body ached right now.

"My name is Sergeant Gitanes, but you can call me G or sarge." Her eyes flicked to the commando standing beside him, a man with strands of wispy red hair peeking from under his helmet. "Salem, the comm working?"

Salem stood at attention. "Yes, Sarge, I've made contact with the Major." Piper tensed. Just as he hoped, the major had survived. They desperately needed her leadership. The sergeant had done okay so far, but she looked more uncertain than confident the longer they failed to make contact. Without the major in command, this mission would probably go much worse than it already had. Not that their current situation was good, but being alive had to be a step in the right direction.

G nodded and pressed a finger on the activation switch on her helmet comm. "Gitanes to Major V, over."

"Go ahead, Sergeant." It was the major's voice all right. Piper wanted to yelp with relief, but held back.

"What's your situation?" asked the major.

"Two dead. The others bruised but fully functional. The passenger survived intact." The sergeant's eyes flitted briefly to him, then her attention went back to studying their surroundings. She seemed to expect something would be here. Piper sensed he hadn't been told everything about this mission.

Major Slim acknowledged the report then continued. "The other pods have reported in. They are vectoring to position. According to our locators you are five klicks from my position."

The sergeant nodded. "We'll rendezvous within the hour."

"Make it forty-five minutes."

"Acknowledged. Gitanes out."

Sergeant Gitanes turned to face the commandos, her expression stern her shoulders back. "Alright, gentlemen, Mr. Cleaner, let's pack up the rations, extra energy packs for the weapons, and prepare to move out. We have a quick march ahead of us, and while we may be banged up we're not down for the count yet. Understood?"

A chorus of "Aye, aye, Sergeant" was followed by a flurry of activity as the pod supplies were retrieved and stored in field packs by three of the burly commandos while the fourth conducted scans of the area.

The soldier identified as Salem used the portable scanner to confirm the Major's coordinates and determine the best route to take. Piper couldn't see any way that looked easier than any other. The rugged terrain was dotted with four to five foot jagged peaks of black lava rock separated by narrow valleys. In order to navigate to the Major's position they would have cross the lava fields. There appeared to be no other option. It would be easy to lose sight of each other after they made it over each peak and down the other side.

The sergeant soon had them clambering over the rocks grunting, swearing, and sweating, the ground beneath their boots trembling with frequent minor quakes as they hiked over the rough terrain.

Piper was grateful he'd decided to wear armored gloves or his hands would have soon been scarred and bleeding.

After fifteen minutes, his breath coming in gasps, Piper was more exhausted than he had ever been in his entire life. He wondered if he would survive this death march.

Looking up at the gray sky with its boiling clouds of ash mingled with the orange fire from active volcanoes, he realized it would be dark soon on this desolate moon. He hoped they'd be at their rendezvous point before then, because he didn't relish the idea of trying to hike over this landscape in the dark.

Suddenly a far more intense quake made him fall to his belly riding the waves of energy as the ground undulated beneath him, tossing him about as if he were a rag doll. A sudden yell of terror echoed through the air, followed by a scream; then silence as the ground at last settled beneath him.

Moving forward Piper managed to grip the sharp edges of the volcanic mini peak in front of him and drag himself with his gloved hands and pull himself up the slope to peer over the top.

Ahead, along a ridge on the other side, stood three of the commandos huddled in a group, their attention focused downward. They weren't moving. What could they be looking at? He hadn't seen any valleys or canyons...his heart froze when he realized a crevasse must have opened during that last earthquake. What if...? He shuddered.

Piper had an unsettling feeling in his gut. "What's happened?" he called to them.

One of the soldiers looked back at him, the commando's expression unreadable. "The Sarge is dead," he said simply.

Piper lost his grip on the rock and slid to the bottom of the slope. Oh, crap, we're in serious trouble.

Chapter Eight

"If you got 'em, smoke 'em."
– Final words of Champion Pelt, leader of the manufacturing planet Rolling Papers, before he expelled the smoke from his last cigarette and then died, aged two hundred and seventy five.

WITH FORTY-EIGHT SECONDS remaining before the two ships were to collide, the rented Lushite vessel finished cycling it's faster than light drive engine and disappeared from the system. The commandos shuttle exploded and was blown into atoms when it reached the position where the Lushite intergalactic ship had been. The resulting explosion was so violent, that if someone had been nearby they would see quite a light show. A few stray comets and asteroids were consumed in the radioactive energy cloud, which would continue to expand for millennia or two.

Two weeks later (local time) the L.S.S. Whiskey Bottle re-entered the system. This time, a heavily-armed probe ship flown by Captain Drive went ahead to detect and address any threats in advance of the mother ship.

"To anyone occupying the system, please respond to our hail." Brain made the announcement and repeated it at regular intervals. No reply was forthcoming.

"Brain, any sign of another ship?" Brain had changed its eye color to turquoise. Cyber thought about saying something about the change since the new color looked nice, but decided the AI didn't need its ego stroked.

"No, not this time."

Cyber snorted derisively. "Like last time you mean?"

"Sorry, captain, I missed detecting the shuttle because someone changed its identification signature to disguise it as a comet. I didn't penetrate the deception until they were too close for comfort. I've now adjusted my scanners to compensate for ships pretending to be comets or meteors or other non-humanoid phenomena."

Cyber chuckled grimly. "Three hundred on-line game pods off line, sixty injuries for abrasions and cuts in the ensuing panic, a run on the snacks and soda supply, waiting for the central game matrix repairs, and me having to listen to that mindless dolt, Smokey Cigarillo complaining about the soda flood in her cabin. Yeah, too close for comfort all right. I warn you, Brain, it better not happen again."

"We could use Smokey you know," the AI suggested. The smoker had stayed on the Whiskey Bottle.

Good thing, thought Cyber. Bad enough she stinks up the mother ship with her burning tobacco leaves.

"Oh, I plan to use her don't you worry, my AI friend."

Brain was right of course. Smokey would be the perfect patsy. A mind scan had already betrayed her plans to start a war so that this "Jal" fellow could take over this galaxy. The one thing the mind probe hadn't revealed was how she planned to start the war. Regardless, he and his boss' had other designs for this galaxy.

Cyber changed course by waving a hand over the motion interface on the control board in front of him. They were to rendezvous with the Whiskey Bottle in orbit around Winston. Smokey told him an emissary from the vice-president would meet them there, and then together they would travel to some cloaked planet.

Cyber smiled to himself at the thought of a cloaked (or did she say hidden?) planet. What nonsense. These special bodies she said were moons were actually planetoids; there was no hidden planet. These people were myth believers. Fools.

"Any idea who tried to destroy us?" Cyber said changing the subject.

"No, but my readings indicate the vessel's dimensions and probable passenger compliment is a military configuration. The ship was small but heavily armed, and the device used to blow the shuttles energy drive crystal was a military grade aluminum based explosive."

Military grade explosives? Interesting. He often dreamed of being in a realistic version of a first person shooter platform. He suppressed a shiver of excitement at the thought of the possible shoot 'em up action. "Any signs of the crew?"

"None, Captain, but extrapolating the vessel's course to its probable point of origin, I discovered the ship mostly likely originated from one of the two moons Smokey told us about. The ones that are supposedly the satellites of the so-called hidden planet."

Cyber rose to his feet and walked to the auto dispenser at the rear of the bridge. After pushing a button on the front of the dispenser, a cold can of grape soda appeared on the materialization pad. Probe ships didn't carry gamer pods. They were designed for only a few hours, so they didn't carry enough supplies for an extended trip, either. An excess amount of supplies were considered wasteful.

"Which moon?" he asked expecting Brain to say Winston.

"Ashtray, naturally."

Cyber's heart skipped a beat when he recalled Smokey's briefing about the two moons. Ashtray's surface was primordial volcanic rock; the inner core unsettled resulting in frequent quakes. Volcanoes appeared unexpectedly spewing toxic gases into the atmosphere. While the air was mostly breathable, the moon's surface would not support life for an extended period. In contrast, Winston was a paradise of green fields, colorful flowers, and warm bodies of water, making it the perfect habitat for a variety of life forms from birds to fish to herds of grass-eating antelope-like animals. There were no predators. Winston would be ideal for colonization by humanoids, but so far no humanoids taken up residence. At least none the smokers knew of.

"Brain, I think this has just become a rescue mission."

***

Two weeks ago (local time)

The floor was cool under Piper's fingertips and the side of his face pressed against its surface. He discovered he was lying face down on something hard yet soft at the same time. The stench of sulfur was gone, replaced by clean, fresh air. Piper sucked the good air into his lungs then coughed. The light level was brighter than it had been seconds before. Raising his head, he shielded his eyes with one hand to gaze at his surroundings.

He was in some kind of room with bright green walls whose brilliance made his eyes hurt.

Piper realized there were bodies scattered all around him. As his eyesight adjusted, he recognized them as the commandos. All of the commandos.

Even the ones who had disappeared into crevasses, or been burned up by lava flows—including their commanding officer, Major V, who had reportedly died in a rock slide.

On the surface of the rugged moon, their numbers had begun to dwindle as the hostile environment assaulted them over and over. Within a couple of days, Piper and two commandos were all that remained. But just as all seemed lost, he was overcome by dizziness and blacked out. He finally woke up here—wherever here was. But he had no sense of how much time had passed.

His heart began to pound when it dawned on him the Sergeant might be here. Slowly he rose until his weight rested on his hands and knees; his breath came in gasps his head swam. After the dizziness passed, he finally managed to stand on his shaky legs.

Making his way amongst the unconscious warriors, he soon found the sergeant laying her on back with her eyes closed. Her chest rose and fell with each shallow breath. She was alive.

Piper dropped to his knees beside her and used his fingers to gently tap Sergeant Gitanes on her left cheek. Clearing his throat, which was dry from the moon's superheated atmosphere he'd just left, he managed to coax a few hoarse words from between his dry lips. "Sergeant...it's Piper...wake up..."

"That isn't going to do much good," said an eerily familar voice.

"Brain?"

"Who do you think it would be...a Belmont pick bird?" Brain said, referring to a bird on Belmont III that gathered tobacco leaves in its beak from plants growing atop ten-mile high mountain peaks. Brain was disguised as an eyeball, but the iris was the light brown color of peanut butter.

Piper shook his head and coughed. His body sagged and he nearly lost consciousness.

A sudden frailty enveloped his body like none he'd ever experienced. What's happened to me? he wondered.

"Don't be concerned, Piper. The weakness you're experiencing will pass in a couple of hours. I was surprised when you awoke before the commandos. They are in far better physical condition than you."

Piper nodded and smiled weakly. "I grew up on Kristal II."

"Ahhh...that explains it."

The gravity of the planets in the Kristal system were twice that of other planets in the galaxy. This meant Piper's bones, muscles, and cartilage were naturally stronger than humanoids from other worlds. The vice president had sent a commando unit made up exclusively of Dirt-origin soldiers. Human physiology may be weak, but humans were fearless fighters who would sacrifice themselves if need be to complete a mission. Many said these humanoids were the perfect soldiers. The dividing line between bug-nut crazy and reckless bravery could sometimes be razor thin.

"When will the others regain consciousness?"

"I estimate within two hours. But I have a slight dilemma." The Brain's tone registered his uncertainty.

Piper rarely heard a Brain who wasn't overly confident, so this was something special. In fact he had never met anyone who said they had experienced anything but arrogant condemnation from a Brain.

"What's the problem?"

"I must decide whether to transport all of you to Four now, or wait until the Lushite ship returns."

Piper frowned at an unseen spot on the snow-white ceiling, hoping the AI could see his annoyance. "Brain, what are you talking about?" A knot of anger formed in Piper's belly. It was as if Brain was being purposefully obtuse.

"It's awkward..." began the AI. "You see I'm not the Brain that travelled with you and the commandos to this moon. I'm Herman Pug's AI. Dr. Pug ordered me to bring you all here—to save you."

Piper swallowed what little saliva left in his mouth and considered the Brain's words. This meant they would get past the shield that hid Four. The mystery planet was real. He considered pinching himself to see if he was still asleep but knew it would only hurt. This place, this Brain, his heat-scorched armor...it was all real, very real. And so were the commandos lying unconscious on the deck of this chamber.

"What does Dr. Pug want from us?" asked Piper, uncertain he really wanted an answer.

"Dr. Pug will have to explain."

OK, thought Piper, now we just have to get to Four. "You mentioned something about transporting us to Four. How do you propose to accomplish this?"

"The same way I transported all of you here."

"Which reminds me, where is here?"

Brain sighed. "We are located inside a mass teleport way station on Ashtray."

Piper sucked in a breath. His heart beat faster. They had landed on the wrong moon. How was this possible? The major had been quite adamant this was the proper moon before they ejected in the escape pods and set the ship on a course away from them...

"Brain, what happened to our shuttle?"

"As I tried to explain the Lushite ship engaged their star drive to escape before the shuttle exploded in an fruitless attempt to destroy it. The Lushite intergalactic vessel will be in the system again in two-point-three hours."

Now Piper was thoroughly confused. Brain's explanations weren't working for him.

I was as if something important were missing from this puzzle. "But, Brain, I don't understand. We're on the wrong moon, and our shuttle was a flying bomb sent to destroy the Lushite ship that I detected." Piper shuffled around the room shaking his head. "I need a drink. Something cold. And a chair." He nodded, his eyes locked on the glowing white plasti-steel floor. "Sitting down. That's the thing to do," he muttered.

He yelped his surprise when he nearly stepped into a cherry red plasti-steel chair and matching side table that had suddenly popped into existence directly in his path. On the table rested a can of his favorite root beer, dripping with beads of perspiration. "Brain! Warn me next time."

"You're welcome."

Piper cheeks grew warm. Brain was quite right, he had been rude. As his mother used to say, "Even AI's have feelings." "Sorry, Brain, it startled me is all." The AI didn't respond. "Don't transport us yet, regardless of what Dr. Pug told you. I have to get this straight before we go anywhere. Besides, I'm as confused as you can get, I thought—"

"You aren't supposed to think, Piper," said feminine voice from behind him.

Piper's hand began to tremble around the can of soda and his breathing became more rapid as fear generated a knot in his belly.

"Brain, I thought you said they'd be out for another couple of hours..."

"I was wrong."

Yeah, you pile of diodes and macro circuits, no kidding.

Piper turned to look in the direction of the voice and saw the major had managed to sit up near a wall, her back now resting against its smooth surface. Her features were drawn and her eyes were sunken in their sockets. "Hello, Major, glad to see you're awake."

Her eyes travelled up and down his lean frame. "You look none the worse for wear yourself, Piper." She shuffled her bottom to the right and winced as if in pain.

He wanted to say for a person who fell into a crevasse she, too, appeared better than expected but he held his tongue. His sixth sense told him he should keep any further opinions and speculations to himself. Hidden agendas were everywhere—including his own. He wondered how much Major Slim had heard of his conversation with Brain.

Swallowing hard he moved across the room and knelt next to the Major. Placing a hand on her shoulder he said, "You OK?"

Smiling weakly she nodded. "It only hurts when I cough."

Though it was the oldest joke in the galaxy Piper chuckled. "Brain brought us here. He saved us under orders from Dr. Herman Pug."

"Doctor who?" asked the major. The puzzled expression on her dirty face made Piper actually believe she didn't know who he was talking about. How odd. Maybe she wasn't supposed to meet Dr. Pug? How can that be right?

Piper patted her arm gently. "Don't worry about it. All will become clear as soon as we get out of here." Piper stood and looked up at the ceiling. "Brain, can you transport all of us out of here?"

"Yes. Immediately," Brain added before Piper could ask.

"Good." But should he ask the AI to transport them now, or wait until the commandos were awake, or wait for the Lushties to return? Now he understood Brain's earlier dilemma more fully. But then caution seemed unnecessary. Brain would transport them to Four. The Lushites were no doubt upset about being attacked by a suicide bomb so it was probably a bad idea to stick around and wait for them. And he doubted the commandos special skills would be needed with Dr. Pug and his Purple. What was the worst that could happen?

"I've given it some thought, Brain, and I think you should transport us now."

"No!" protested the Major, her voice stronger now.

Piper looked at her. Beads of sweat peppered her brow and the pain on her face reflected her losing struggle to get off the floor. Evidently her strength hadn't fully returned yet. All the more reason to get her to the planet and possible medical aid. This way station didn't seem to have even the most basic amenities in that regard.

"Ignore her, Brain, transport all of us now."

After what seemed like an eternity, a tingling sensation that ran from the top of his head down to his toes then back again made him want to giggle. Then the room around him became fuzzy, hard to see, followed by darkness. Finally, all physical sensation disappeared until it was replaced by warmth from what could only be a sun, and a terrifyingly loud whine as a bolt of superheated energy zipped past his right ear.

Pain.

Touching his ear gingerly with his fingertips, he realized the outer edge of his ear had been singed by an energy weapon's beam. A nearby explosion made him drop to his belly and bury his head under his arms. He realized the ground beneath him was covered in green grass. He could smell the chlorophyll, tainted by an odor of burnt ozone.

He looked up when a bloodcurdling yell, he could only describe as a war cry, came from somewhere in front of him. He spotted a six-foot tall, chocolate-colored bear (it looked like a toy bear more than it did an organic one) striding across the field of flowers, trees, and grass, its coal-black button eyes intent on something in the distance behind him. His eyes flitted around the field, and he could hardly believe what he was seeing.

Racing across the grass and flowers was an untold number of six-foot teddy bears of all colors of the rainbow—from yellow to blue to bright green—wielding energy weapons and firing indiscriminately toward a hill comprised of hover car-sized boulders.

His heart skipped a beat when one of the teddy bears headed his way suddenly threw back its head and emitted a terrifying roar while waving a blast rifle in the air. The bear-like features were twisted in anger. Suddenly it charged across the field straight at him.

Hiding his head under his arms again he realized what had happened. Damn that Brain. He dropped us into the middle of a war zone!

And that bear-thing meant to kill him.

Chapter Nine

"A game a minute is needed to win It."
– Game Master Blog Armageddon, first champion of The Gamers Alliance who lost his title when a glitch in the game program revealed he cheated. His execution occurred the next day after several failed appeals.

TRIXIE AND PETER ARRIVED BY HOVER CAB at the spaceport to find the chief engineer for the Gamers Alliance, Beta Tester, waiting for them at the passenger drop-off area at the front of the main terminal.

"That'll be fifty-seven credits, or next time you walk," said the auto-driver coldly, before unlocking the rear passenger compartment doors.

Trixie's brow furrowed. In the old days, when she was CEO of Heavenly Sky Burger, she would have bought the cab company, fired the auto-driver, and had him disassembled and sold for scrap if it dared speak to her so rudely. But these days, her trim figure and relaxed retirement had given her a different outlook on life, and machines and people who annoyed her. She ignored the impudent device and stepped out onto the curb.

"Peter," she said without looking back. "Take care of the driver."

Pasting a wide grin on her lips, she motioned to slap hands with her friend, Beta, who was waiting for them on the spaceport walkway, but he kept his hands folded behind his bulbous body. "Beta Tester, as I live and breath. How are you and the pit crew doing these days?" she said.

Beta's wrinkled jowls wobbled, and his sunken, forest-green eyes, set deep in his sagging gray flesh, glared at her. She'd been unable to discern his age since she met him, but she assumed he was quite old. "Hello, Mrs. Pug, welcome to the spaceport. I have readied the Flash-O-Matic for your trip. Which I think is a very reckless idea."

Trixie's grin faded and she regarded the engineer to determine if he was serious. Why was he being so formal? They'd been friends for years, and in all that time he'd always called her Trix. Why the change?

She dropped her hand to her side when it was evident he had refused the traditional Snackcake greeting. She shrugged, brushing off his rebuff. "Let's walk," she said with a wave of one hand.

Her eyes flicked back to Peter, who was still tearing a verbal strip off the auto-driver and so far had gotten the fare reduced to thirty-five credits. Ten more to go, she thought with a small smile passing over her lips. That's my boy.

Once inside the terminal, Trixie led the way to a juice and vegetable drink bar. She ordered two glasses of celery and carrot, with a twist of lemon, then carried the drinks to a table Beta had selected for them. Given he was much shorter than her, once seated his chair rose until he was at eye level with her Trixie placed the two drinks between them on the plasti-steel surface.

Beta grumbled a weak protest at her choice—he preferred caffeine raspberry—then took a sip of the fresh juice. Setting the glass on the table, he locked eyes with her. "I mean what I say," he said.

Trixie smiled in an attempt to shatter his icy demeanor. "I would expect nothing less." She took a brief swallow of juice, then rested her elbows on the table and leaned closer to him. She had lowered her voice so as not to attract the attention of the curious ears around her.

One thing that annoyed her about Snackcakians was their predilection for listening in on the conversations of others. The Snackcakians with their squat statures and bigger ears than humans made them the perfect stealth race. Low and listening was in their DNA. And they had cheeks that puffed out like squirrels where they stored their snack foods for times when they were hungry. Their food habits had initially made Trixie and Peter uncomfortable at times but they had grown more comfortable around these beings eventually.

Since she and Peter, as humans, already attracted attention, privacy could be an issue. "Listen, Beta, my lumpkin," she added the term of affection she used to use when they were dating to soften his wrinkled hide, "you and I have a past, but I have to do this. Herman is still Peter's father."

Beta looked away and a frown deepened the wrinkles on forehead. "So it's true. Herman's still alive. Even after all this time." His voice contained an edge of bitterness.

"So I'm told, but the source of this information is less than reliable." She shrugged again. "Truthfully the source is far more unreliable than less."

Beta turned to eye her with one eyebrow cocked. "Who provided this information?"

Trixie's cheeks grew warm. Even she knew the idea of taking a trip based on the word of an alien liar was a little crazy. "The Purple. Mickelott."

Beta had just taken a sip of the juice and started to gag. His eyes almost bugged out of their sockets.

He sputtered and coughed. "The Purple! That lying sack of gelatinous alien goo! You're taking his word that Herman's alive in the hope your son will have a parental relationship? He's a dead man...more than a thousand years have passed in your old galaxy." He shook his head causing his sagging jowls to sway as if in a breeze. "This is nuts." His eyes shot to lock on hers as his generous mouth formed a grim line. "You and Peter have worked hard to lose weight, you're beautiful inside and out..." His words trailed off and his eyes brimmed with tears. "What's the use? I'm through with you." He stood and walked away, leaving a stunned Trixie alone at the table.

Peter walked up to the table, his attention on the retreating chief engineer. After sitting down he looked at his mother. "Problem?"

Trixie nodded. What a terrible thing, she thought. I had no idea Beta was in love with me all these years. Pity I didn't love him back but I don't. "Yes. Our trip will be delayed slightly." They couldn't leave the Gamers Alliance galaxy without a chief engineer. The Flash-o-Matic 3000 could be very finicky, and the last thing they needed was another trip to a strange universe. One such trip was enough for a lifetime.

Trixie ran through a mental checklist of engineers that could manage the ship. Six were dead, three were in prison, and two had disappeared into black holes. Besides Beta, that left one possible candidate. She mentally cringed as she pictured the four-limbed, crimson-skinned alien—a former security officer who, since arriving in this galaxy had attained several degrees, including one in advanced propulsion systems. Unfortunately, Trixie and her former bodyguard had parted on less than amiable terms.

Regardless they needed Cherry Bomb. She was their only hope.

***

A nearby explosion showered Piper with soil, grass, and the remains of flowers blown apart by the force of the blast. Stealing a glance to his right he saw Major Slim was crawling on her belly across the field trying to get to cover provided by a four-foot high outcropping of rocks jutting from the grass. Thankfully the major still had her pulse rifle on her back. He, on the other hand, had lost his weapon.

He swiveled his head to look behind him and spotted a six-foot tall black and white stuffed panda wearing battle armor similar to the type worn by the Order of The Gold Leaf Tobacco commandos. With a laser rifle in its paws, the bear was shooting beams of superheated energy at the teddy bears, who had abandoned their wild charge when several of their number had been cut down, including the one that had been racing directly at Piper. There were heaps of charred bear stuffing scattered everywhere. It seemed pandas were better soldiers than teddy bears.

So far none of the still unconscious commandos lying on their backs scattered across the field had been hit by rifle fire, but given the intensity of the battle, the odds were they would be shot eventually. Piper knew he had to do something before that happened.

When he realized the pandas were redirecting their fire away from him, he rose and, crouching low to make himself a smaller target, scurried across the field, running toward the same rocky outcropping the major was headed for.

They arrived simultaneously and together took up a position, putting the rocks between themselves and the pandas. There was still the very real threat posed by the teddy bears, but they seemed to have been split into two groups to the right and left of their position. They were occupied with concentrating their weapons fire on the panda's fixed position amongst the boulders.

"Major," gasped Piper his breathing jagged from the run across the field. Not that fear wasn't also a factor in his being short of breath. "Do you know where we are?"

The major was also breathing hard. "No. But please find that Brain so I can strangle it."

"I'm with you, Major, but right now we have to rescue your soldiers."

Her eyes flicked to him. "Yes, of course, you're right. Any ideas?"

"I'm still wearing my portable comm unit. I can try to contact the Lushite ship. It might be in orbit by now."

The major's body tensed and she scowled. Her eyes betrayed her view that it might be better to fight than retreat. It was well known the commandos preferred death to dishonor. Retreating wasn't part of their unofficial code of honor. Finally, after considering the options she said, her body language reading albeit reluctantly, "OK. Give it a try. But if you fail we fight. Agreed?"

Piper nodded, sighed, then sucked in a breath. Then this better work. Expelling the air from his lungs he tapped the activation node on his earpiece. "Piper Cleaner to anyone who can hear me."

He waited. No response. His heart sank. "Piper Cleaner calling anyone, anywhere."

Nothing. He wondered how many shots it took to drain a power cell in a pulse rifle.

Third time lucky. "Piper Cleaner to anyone. We need help."

"Well, why didn't you say so?" came the immediate reply.

"I'm sorry?" Piper sputtered. "Who is this?"

"It's me Brain. I thought you were enjoying yourselves."

Anger pinched Piper's stomach muscles. "Enjoying what? Being shot at and nearly killed? What would make you think that?"

A sudden bolt of energy sheared a piece off the rock to his right, showering them with dust. He could feel the wave of heat against his skin. "Brain! Get us out of here!"

"OK, OK," said the AI. "I've scanned your position and there are twenty-one humanoids on the surface. Is this correct?"

Piper covered his eyes when a second pulse blast, only closer this time, sheared off more of their limited cover. "Yes! Just do it! Now!"

The now familiar tingling sensation associated with the transport device used by Brain returned. Piper next found himself standing on a gray, plasti-steel pad in a barren, gray room. The lighting was dim, so his eyesight adjusted quickly to his new surroundings. A sense of relief washed over him when he saw the commandos were scattered at his feet all around him; then he realized Major Slim was not among them.

"Brain!" His words echoed off the surrounding walls. "Where's the major!"

"What's a major?" asked the Brain.

Good thing AI's memory cells are stored in tamper-proof facilities, thought Piper gritting his teeth, or I'd tear out his memory circuits one by one. Taking a deep breath he kept his voice even. "Brain, this is no time for games—"

"That's where you're wrong."

Suddenly Piper was again gripped by the tingling sensation and the room around him disappeared in a burst of light.

When the transport beam ceased he almost fell over. The floor beneath his feet was moving back and forth. A warm breeze tinged with salt washed over his face filling his senses. Finally his vision cleared and he discovered the moving floor was in reality the deck of a vessel looking over a choppy blue-green sea. The sound of a loud snap, like the crack of a whip, made him look up to see two large canvas sails attached to wooden masts filled by the wind.

Where has the AI sent me this time?

A loud explosion erupted near him, the force of the blast slamming him face down on the wooden deck. Ouch.

A spray of salt water and wooden splinters rained down on him. Choking and coughing from the rush of acrid smoke and the bitter water that invaded his nose and mouth, he rolled onto his back. His eyes fluttered open in time to see one of the masts had been shattered half way up its length. The massive, heavy looking masthead had begun to fall toward him. It seemed to be coming at slow motion. His heart froze when he realized when it landed it would crush him like an insect. Is this what your impending death looks like? he wondered.

"Brain!" he yelled and averted his eyes, covering them with his arm. But nothing happened. No transport. Fear gripped him. His doom appeared inevitable.

A sickening thud followed by a cracking sound made him tremble. This is it.

Silence. The smell of smoke filled his nostrils. The smoke had an acrid, unpleasant odor unlike tobacco smoke which soothed shattered nerves on a daily basis (slogans, gotta love 'em), but smoking would have to wait for now. I can't believe I just said that. It's been too long been since I had a cig, he thought. Instinctively he licked his dry lips.

Removing his arm from his eyes he saw the shattered mast lay at an angle a couple of feet above his head, the rail of the vessel itself interrupting its path to his destruction. The heavy sails and tangled rigging hung around him, enveloping him like a shroud. What a cheery thought.

Scrambling to his feet, Piper made his way from under the sail into the smoky air. The deck beyond was littered with bloody bodies and piece of bodies violently blown apart by whatever weapon had been used to bring down the mast.

Russ Crossley

Walking back to the rail he saw another vessel, its twin sails billowing in the wind. The attacking ship had steered an intercept course with numerous guns ports open along its wooden hull.

A half dozen puffs of smoke erupted from the side the approaching vessel, followed by several explosions around him. Two strikes below the water line caused his ship to rock violently, nearly forcing him off his feet, but he managed to grab the rail in time and hang on. Three enormous pillars of water shot into the air next to the ship. Finally an explosion on an upper deck above him blew a large hole in the wooden planks, sending body parts and shards of wood flying in all directions—some even over the rail into the sea below. Piper ducked behind the sail to avoid the razor sharp wood shards raining down on him.

After the exploded missiles finished, Piper stepped out from behind the sail. The crew of the attacking vessel was now close enough so he could see them clearly. His jaw dropped. They were dressed in the clothing of what used to be called "seafaring buccaneers" like he'd only seen in historical vids.

Ancient Dirt pirates? How did that make any sense out here at the edge of the galaxy?

Looking around, he realized the commandos hadn't been brought with him this time. He recalled the major had already been sent somewhere else, or was she still at the battle of the bears?

He pondered the problem. Didn't Brain say something about games?

Freezing, he realized the key to what had been happening to him. Games?

He nearly slapped himself. How could I be so blind? This is a game! It had to be the answer.

It was the only scenario that made any sense of warring toy bears, and ancient pirate ships dueling on the high seas. But what about that mess on Ashtray? The experience on a rocky lump of molten rock certainly wasn't any game, or at least it hadn't felt like one unless someone enjoyed being shaken and baked on an unstable volcanic moon. There was no accounting for taste, but the experience seemed most unlikely for even the most ardent gamer.

"Brain!" The only sounds were the rush of the ocean by the hull and the pop from black powder rifles being fired at him by the crew of the attacking ship. "Answer me now, you pile of scrap diodes and tainted memory gels." He dipped his head when steel shot ricocheted off the rail and punched holes in the sail. Good thing those pirates are poor shots.

"Alright. You don't have to yell at me."

"Really? I should be all calm about you putting the commandos and me in harm's way. I don't think so."

"I'm sorry," said the Brain, "I'm confused. I thought you enjoyed these games. Frankly, I find them a bit tedious and dull, but then I'm no measure of taste. After all alternate reality is my lifestyle."

Piper considered the AI's words and was about to respond when an explosion threw him to the deck knocking him unconscious.

Chapter Ten

"Fast food is a disease that must be eradicated along with anyone who opposes us. Smoking is the future. Smoking is more important than life. We must roll over the fatties."
– Excerpt from a speech by the President of Galaxy Tobacco the day before the emperor fled into exile.

THE HOVER CAB SPED AWAY after Trixie paid the bill without question. Peter had protested but she silenced her son with a look. She gazed up at the two hundred and seventy story glass and plasti-steel tower they stood in front of until it disappeared into fluffy white clouds. The wide sidewalk was busy with hover chairs, the occupants of which steered around them with frowns and glares on their pudgy features as they floated past them.

Over ninety percent of the residents of Snackcakes III were descendants of exiles from the fast food galaxy. Many were obese, though greasy fried foods were getting harder to come by, so, much to their dismay some were losing weight.

Tensions had been rising for some time due to food shortages, and even if she wasn't leaving to visit Herman, Trixie had been considering leaving before the start of a revolution. She shuddered at the thought of what would happen if the fast foodies started to miss meals. Her memories of her own hunger pains were like opening fresh wounds in her soul.

"Why are we here? I thought we were leaving to visit father," said Peter.

Trixie looked at her son and a brief smile passed her lips. "If we don't have an engineer for the ship we're not going anywhere. Do you recall what it was like in the garbage universe?" Peter's cheeks grew red and the arrogance in his body language evaporated before her eyes. His shoulders sagged like a balloon after the air had been let out.

"Alright, let's go find the one person who might be able to get us off this rock and safely to the fast food galaxy."

An obese woman in her hover chair came up short beside them and stared at Trixie her beady eyes wide. "Did you say something about travelling to the fast food galaxy?" she said.

Trixie shifted her attention to the woman and pasted the fat woman with her best let's-all-be-pals grin. "No, of course not, how could we travel there? We're not Lushites." Trixie chuckled.

The woman grinned and chuckled as well. "Yes. How silly of me. I must have misheard you." She sped away, her hover chair humming, without looking back, much to Trixie's relief.

That was too close. I could have triggered an incident. We live in difficult times.

Now she was more convinced than ever the sooner they vacated the planet the better. "Com'on, son, let's get off the street." She led the way through the glass doors into the building's lobby.

A Snackcakian security guard sat behind a desk on a raised dais set against a gray plasti-steel wall separating two corridors, one on either side of the security station, each containing banks of high speed lifts. Other than the lone guard, the lobby was devoid of people, plants, or any other amenities, living or otherwise.

The guard, evidently male (Snackcakian male's noses are six inches longer than females), had his sky blue eyes fixed on a vid screen on the desk in front of him. Trixie, with Peter beside her, approached the desk and stood looking up at the guard who didn't seem to notice her. She tried to gain his attention by loudly clearing her throat but he still didn't look in her direction. After casting Peter a disparaging glance she decided on a new tactic.

After stepping to one side of the desk she cupped her mouth with her hands and yelled, "Help! Fire!"

The guard leapt to his feet then vaulted over the desk to land on all fours like a cat his eyes flitted around the lobby seeking the danger. "Did someone say fire?" he said his voice husky.

"How did you know?" whispered Peter.

Trixie smiled knowingly. "Experience, son. Experience."

Stepping forward she tapped the guard on the shoulder then stepped back. The guard stood upright his blaster drawn and pointed at Trixie. "Who goes there?" he said.

Trixie chuckled. "You win your bet? Ya know on the game you were watching on your screen."

The guard hesitated then slowly lowered his blaster. He eyed Trixie then his gaze flitted to Peter then back to her. After holstering his weapon he said, "Very funny." His eyes narrowed. "Aren't you one of those humans? From Dirt is it?"

"Yes, me and my son, Peter, here are both from Dirt. We're looking for Dr. Bomb."

"Bomb, huh?" He walked around the desk and climbed the two steps at the back of the dais. Sitting in his chair again he tapped the screen with one finger. "There's a Dr. Cherry Bomb who works for Lick'em-Tick'em Propulsion Systems on the two-hundred and fifteenth floor."

"That'd be her," said Trixie. She made a faux salute then nodded to Peter to follow her to the lifts. "Well, it's been a slice."

"Hold on, not so fast, human. I have to call upstairs to ask permission. Then once they give the okay I need to swipe both your palm prints into the system so you can pass the security checkpoints." His eyes crinkled at the corners. "If you don't wait until you're cleared, the checkpoint alarms will go off and you might be hurt. You may not be aware but some checkpoints are in high security areas and have disintegration rays that will make a very bad day for an intruder."

Trixie considered her options. The guard was right disintegration could indeed hurt. It might be better to play along for now. "Oh, OK, let's see what they say," she said, forcing herself to sound casual. A knot of tension formed in her stomach. She had a bad feeling in her gut about how Cherry might react to their presence. Her only hope was there would be intermediaries between her and her old friend to intercede in case things got ugly. The worst case was if Cherry herself responded to the news Trixie wanted to see her. Anyway you looked at this, it was risky to let this guard announce her.

"Is this standard procedure?" asked Peter before the guard could make the call.

The guard appeared uncertain and he hesitated just long enough so that Trixie decided to follow her son's lead by playing a hunch. "I'm not so sure," she said. "Something smells rotten on Snackcakes III." Trixie eyed the guard with her best 'I'll-kick-your-butt' look. "Who told you to delay us?"

The guard swallowed and his hands trembled as beads of perspiration appeared on his forehead. Her question had found a soft spot. Time to apply even greater pressure to the opening she'd created. "You better tell us or we'll report you to the city enforcers for violation of our alien rights."

After the Lushites and human exiles arrived on Snackcake, there were interspecies tensions. But soon the new arrivals began to add much needed funds into the local economy and the mounting success caused the Snackcakian rulers to pass strict anti-discrimination laws to protect the aliens, and their own treasurery, from harm. The consequences of breaking these laws could be very serious, including a death sentence in some of the more serious instances.

Not surprisingly Trixie's threat had the desired effect. "I'm sorry, but Dr. Bomb ordered me to report anyone asking to see her," said the guard after averting his eyes. "She paid me a lot of credits."

Trixie relaxed her aggressive demeanor. "It's okay. Don't worry; if you allow us to go up unannounced we'll tell her we tricked you. Everyone wins."

The tension in the guard seemed to ebb from the man as his shoulders relaxed. "OK. I'll swipe your palms and then it's like we never met." His pleading eyes looked into Trixie's. "Will that be okay?"

"Yes, of course...whoever you are."

***

When they arrived on the two hundred and fifteenth floor, they were greeted at reception by an alien originally from Guillotine II. She had two extended eyestalks, a wide mouth filled with jagged, razor-sharp teeth, and no hair on her pale green-skinned scalp. Her head was shaped like an upside down eggshell with the little end on top.

Her physiology was basically humanoid in design, except for the eyes, four legs and four arms, and their skin color. The additional appendages made the Guillotineians very efficient multi-taskers and therefore very skilled as receptionists or scientists.

"May I be of assistance?" she said, her voice musical, when Trixie and Peter stepped out of the high-speed lift. The reception area had a wall separating it from the main office areas. A painting of one of the planet's moons, Twinkie, hung on the wall. Against another wall was a brown overstuffed couch with a clear plexi coffee table in front with a short stack of reading pads for waiting visitors to pass the time. A well-lit corridor ran away to a distant door in the other direction.

Trixie offered the dour faced receptionist a brief smile, her hands behind her back. "Yes, you may, we're looking for Dr. Bomb."

The receptionist hesitated then without responding pressed a comm button recessed into the desk next to her elbows. "Security to reception fifteen A. Code Beta Green One."

Trixie froze. What just happen—? She hadn't even finished the thought when two burly, serious-looking men appeared, dressed in the same uniform as the guard in the lobby. They each held a blast pistol in their right hands aimed at them.

Beside her Peter yelped and raised his hands above his head. Trixie smirked keeping her hands behind her back. "Is there a problem?" she said her tone even.

"These two have a bomb," the receptionist said to the taller of the two-armed guards. The other guard had moved to Trixie's left, keeping his weapon trained on them, his eyes watchful for any threatening moves.

"I'm standing right here. As I said, we want to see Dr. Cherry Bomb, the propulsion scientist, I assure you we don't have a bomb."

The taller guard turned to face the receptionist. "Is this true, ma'am?"

The receptionist nodded, her narrow forehead wrinkled and her eyestalks waving indicating she was annoyed. "Yes, they did say something about Dr. Bomb. Aren't you going to search them?"

The taller guard glanced at his partner and they exchanged a look then both holstered their weapons. Turning his attention to Trixie, the taller guard said, "Sorry, Bella here tends to be overly cautious. We've had some incidents." The way he said "incidents" made Trixie think these events—whatever they were—too often involved more imagination than real threats.

"No harm done," Trixie said cheerily. "Perhaps you will escort us to Dr. Bomb's office?"

The guard nodded. "It's the least I can do." With a nod of his head he indicated the other guard could leave. The shorter of the two quickly retreated down the corridor and through the door at the end, closing it behind him.

The taller guard had his multi-use security scanner and comm tool out and was bringing up the location of Dr. Bomb's office. A shadow of doubt crossed his rugged features, then he arched an eyebrow. He put away his scanner and the frown on his massive forehead deepened. "I'm not sure I can take you there," he said finally.

"Why not?' said Peter before Trixie could respond.

"Her office is located in a high security area. An area above my pay grade. An area where visitors are not allowed. Ever."

"What if we go there anyway?" said Peter indignantly.

The guard's eyes narrowed and Trixie saw his fingers drift to the butt of his holstered pistol. "If you intend to ignore our security restrictions then I must kill you here and now. Is this your intention?"

Chapter Eleven

"Games are for the young and the young at heart. So, people, let the games begi—oh, my broken butts!"
– Former Emperor Bud Wiser delivering the opening address to the XIII Gamers Alliance Olympics in 4435, the year Trixie and Peter Pug arrived from the Garbage Collectors Universe and crashed into the Olympic flame, extinguishing it.

PIPER AWOKE IN DARKNESS laying on something soft on his back. Is this a bed perhaps? He shifted his weight a little. The small movement sent a shock of pain through his slight frame. Sucking in a breath and ignoring the pain, he managed to look in the direction of where he thought his feet were to see a sliver of light coming from the bottom of a door.

After releasing his breath with a rush he gritted his teeth and shifted his body again, wincing. His entire body ached, his muscles strained as if someone had smacked him around. Even flexing his toes sent waves of pain through him. Clearing his throat, he realized his mouth and throat were incredibly dry.

He could really use a cigarette right now.

"Hello?" he croaked in the silence. His voice sounded funny, higher-pitched than normal. Where am I?

"How you feelin'?" said the familiar voice of Major Slim. She seemed to be nearby, perhaps in another bed.

"Not good," he said. "Where are you, major?"

"Look to your right."

Piper's eyes slowly adjusted in the darkness until he could make out the shape of an old fashioned, steel-framed bed. Finally the humanoid shape of a woman coalesced as his vision finally adjusted and he saw her eyes peering back at him in the dim light. "You okay?"

When she nodded he realized her movements were somehow restricted. He tried to move his arms and realized he, too, had been strapped to the bed. The real question was why? And who was behind the curtain?

"Where did the Brain send you after we left Ashtray?" Piper asked.

The major grunted. "I ended up in some game called "dance wars"."

"What's that?" Piper smiled to himself. It was hard to imagine Major Slim dancing.

"I'll fill you in on the details later," said the major, her tone dripping with sarcasm. "For now, let's just say I was lucky to get out of there alive." She snorted. "As for where we are now, that's another question. I've been here for a while and you arrived only a few minutes ago. Any ideas who's behind these events?"

"Yes. The Brain told me he served Herman Pug, so I believe Mr. Pug has been engineering these events, not for us but for someone else."

"Is that some kind of joke?" interrupted a man's voice. "Engineering...I'm an engineer...ha, ha...funny."

Piper's tensed causing pain in his shoulders. That had to be... "What are you talking about, Mr. Pug?"

"Do we know each other?"

"No, we've never met; but we have met your AI." Piper pushed through the pain and struggled against the bindings tying him to the bed. Inky blackness crept in from the edges of his vision. He knew he'd pass out soon if he didn't stop fighting, but he had to make this megalomaniac act if he wanted to get to the bottom of whatever was happening to them.

"No! Don't! Stop!" Piper realized Herman didn't wish to harm them. But how had he simulated sore muscles in his and the major's bodies? And where were the other commandos?

"If I stop will you stop?" Piper said between gritted teeth.

"Yes," came the immediate reply.

A sudden burst of light forced him to squeeze his eyes shut. This was followed by the disorienting sensation of being transported he had experienced enough now to be familiar with. When the transport finished, Piper opened one eye and realized he was waist deep in warm water. Sunlight reflected off the smooth-as-glass surface. Opening both eyes he peered into the water around him. It was clear and he could see to the gray and brown sandy bottom. He didn't see signs of fish or other life in evidence. Looking down Piper could see his own pale, pasty flesh. His breath caught in his throat and he froze. I'm naked.

Glancing to his left he saw Major Slim stood next to him, also very much naked. He hurriedly averted his eyes, but not before noticing her washboard stomach and muscular arms and legs. She was in incredible physical condition. "I'm sorry...I..." Stumbling over his words he really didn't know what to say.

Anger grew in his belly. "Brain! Herman Pug! What are you two doing to us? I'm really getting mad now."

Brain's laugh filled the air, and a disembodied white eyeball with a purple iris appeared, hovering over the water a few yards away. Though obviously a hologram, Piper knew immediately who had adopted this persona. "Brain. You better start explaining what's going on before..." What could he really do? Nothing. The AI held all the transporter cards.

Brain's laughter ebbed. "Sorry, but it's just a game. A silly game. I'm told you people like to play games, so I created all these game platforms to welcome you to Four. Herman said it would be fun for you."

"Do I look like I'm having fun?" Piper waved his bare arms in the air. "I'm naked, up to my waist in water, I've been shot at by heavily armed bears, pirates tried to blow me to bits, and I was strapped to a bed in the dark. How would this be fun for anyone?"

"You mean this isn't fun?" said a very surprised-sounding Brain.

Piper thought the AI had somehow malfunctioned, and then he suddenly realized what had happened. "You think we're Lushites," he said. "Don't you?"

"Aren't you?" The eyeball floated toward him until it was too close for comfort. "What would you like to drink? A beer? A whiskey perhaps?"

Piper splashed water at the hologram with his hands forcing it to retreat. Beads of water dripped from his hair. ""I'm not a Lushite. I'm a citizen of the Smokers Republic and I know my rights." For the first time in his life Piper stood up for himself, and by extension, others.

"I'm with my friend," said the major from his left. Piper stayed focused on the AI's holo image. "We're smokers, not boozers or gamers, or whatever else you and Mr. Pug seem to think we are."

"I don't think anything, I'm Herman's AI. He does all the thinking. But never mind that it's not important," said the Brain. "Where is Smokey Cigarillo? Isn't she with you?"

"No, of course not. Who is this person?" asked Piper. He vaguely recalled someone named Smokey in the brief transmitted to him by Vice President Popover but the name hadn't seemed important enough to him at the time to remember the details. He knew a lot of beings named Smokey, the name had been very popular since the Day of the Big Smoke. There were literally millions of beings with that name scattered across the galaxy. How was he supposed to remember one Smokey in particular? Popover could have meant anyone, from a janitor on Ambrosia I, to a cigar roller on Zino II and every planetary system with humanoids in between.

"Smokey Cigarillo. You know the one representing Vice President Popover to the Lushites. They're on the way here right now. We thought they were with you...aren't they?"

"No, we were also sent by the vice-president, but he didn't say anything about this Smokey person or the Lushites. He did tell us we'd meet his contact, and a ship, but he never provided us with names even in the briefing report..." Piper hesitated as it dawned on him what he was saying.

"Brain transport the Major and I out of here and bring the commandos as well. I have a possible answer not only us but for you and Herman as well."

"Sure," replied the Brain, "where do you want to go?"

Interesting, thought Piper. "Where are we now?"

The Brain chuckled. "I created a new look for the Winston way station. What do you think?"

Piper appreciated the expanse of water all around them that appeared to disappear mimicking the curve of a real planet where the sky seemed to merge with the water. It was a truly impressive simulation. "I think it's one heck of a construct but how about you bring back our clothes and create some dry land?"

"No worries."

The water, the sky, and the surroundings shimmered and Piper found himself once again (much to his relief) dressed in his military issue jumpsuit and battle armor and standing on the sandy ground of a barren plain. A warm yellow sun shone on him from a brilliant azure cloudless sky. A thankfully, also clothed Major Slim stood next to him. Glancing around he located the remaining commandos standing in a huddled group blinking in confusion. Surprisingly everyone had their weapons. Reaching over his left shoulder his fingers touched the cool metal of his own pulse rifle. He could appreciate now how soldiers became so obsessed about their weapons. The comfort of even confirming it was there was an almost tobacco-like experience.

He sighed. "Thanks, Brain, this is good."

Piper turned to face the Major who now wore a scowl on her angular features. "I think we've been set up," he said. "I think the vice-president wanted us to attack the Lushite ship hoping it would spark a war."

She only nodded, and the look in her eyes made Piper think Popover had really pissed off the wrong person this time. Now all they had to do was find and convince Smokey Cigarillo and the Lushites what he suspected about the vice president. Then, together, they'd have to devise a plan of their own. And then of course if Trixie and Peter Pug showed up he'd have to convince them of the truth as well, and they'd have to agree to help them if they were to have any chance of convincing Herman to help them.

He smiled to himself. Simple. Right?

***

Trixie grabbed Peter by his arm and dragged him out of hearing range of the burly guard. Once out of earshot she released him. He rubbed his arm where she held him, his youthful features marred by a scowl. "This is not the time to start anything with these people," she said. "Besides we don't even know where her office is exactly, but I'm pretty sure it's not on this floor, or this building for that matter."

Peter's expression eased and his eyes flitted to the guard who watched them with narrow eyes and a determined expression on his tanned features. Turning his attention back to his mother Peter nodded. "I supposed you're right about fighting the guy, but how do you know Cherry's not here?"

"The guard said her lab was located in a high security area. We haven't seen any signs indicating there are any such areas on this floor. In fact I haven't seen any indication of any high security areas in the building at all. We've only been told there are."

Leaving Peter alone Trixie approached the guard a forced smile on her lips. "I understand completely. Why don't you accompany us to the lobby then we'll be on our way?"

The guard nodded uncertainly then led them to the lifts. The receptionist glared at them from behind her desk as they walked past. Trixie had the urge to wave, but decided it was better not to antagonize her further. It would be fun but pointless.

The lift arrived and the three stepped into the car then the doors closed. After arriving at the security desk where Trixie and Peter again swiped their palms under the supervision of the first guard they'd met, the security system recorded they'd exited the building.

The two guards bid them goodbye with terse nods. They were now on the sidewalk standing in front of the Research and Development building where they'd started.

"Alright, mother," Peter said, his tone heavy with sarcasm, "this trip was a complete bust. We're not going to get off this rock any time soon."

Trixie smiled at him after sidestepping an impatient fast-foodie in a hover chair who nearly knocked her over. "That's where you'd be wrong," she said.

Peter chuckled grimly. "Mother, we were basically thrown out and threatened with death...how am I wrong?"

Trixie pulled her portable Intelli-comm unit from her hidden pocket and called up the city street map on the screen. "Voice activation on code, T-one-seven-three-cheese-five-seven-apple-cardboard." Since the Comm Surveillance-Banana Split Ban Act of 4144 user encryption codes had been mandatory on all Intelli-designed portable comm units.

"User approved. Go," replied the comm unit.

"Bring up the address for Dr. Cherry Bomb's lab."

"I already provided that information."

Trixie's eyes flitted to Peter who nodded. A shadow of a frown darkened Trixie's features. "Never mind. Do it again."

The comm unit beeped when the map of this street appeared on the screen. Peering at the address she saw a red line surrounded it. Glancing at the number of the buildings around them he realized what happened. Cherry's lab was under the building. Sure enough the address for the building included the word under in tiny print beneath the address. She'd failed to notice it when she'd first called up the address.

129

The comm unit had been correct it had brought up the same information, but no point it swelling the learning machines already inflated ego any further by telling the device it was right. Intelli-comm's were incredibly arrogant, almost as if they were children of the Brain.

The problem now was how to find the entrance to the lab from the street. She hadn't seen a sign or any indication in the lift car that it went to below street level, or as she suspected, to a sub-basement deep underground. Corporations often had many secret and clandestine projects going on, some for governments, others for not-for-profit research groups, or megalomaniacs bent on planetary domination at the wrong side of the butt.

Given the details the guards provided about the high-level security protocols regarding intruders she suspected they were telling the truth. To come this far only to fail did not sit well with her. She had to find a way around the security measures without being disintegrated. But how?

Wait a minute. Brain. The AI would know how to defeat any security system. But she hated to ask it. When she left the house this morning the Brain seemed overly annoyed they were planning to head for Dirt. A grumpy artificial intelligent interface made for a very bad breakfast. Burnt veggie bacon really tasted awful. But she had to try, or this trip would never happen. And if she did nothing, the trip wouldn't happen regardless. What did she have to lose?

"Peter," she began looking into her son's inquisitive eyes, "not that I want to, but we have to talk to the Brain. He'll know the way into Cherry's lab." She looked away to study the rush of busy commuters and shoppers crowding the busy downtown streets. It was nearing the midday break. The residents—Snackcakians, Fast-Foodies, and other assorted aliens—were anxious to eat or meet in the cafes, juice bars, and alien foods specialty restaurants that dotted this area of the city.

Her eyes narrowed and her slight frame tightened as anger surged through her. "I suspect the Brain knew all about these roadblocks we've been experiencing. I think he wanted us to fail."

Chapter Twelve

Clouds are best. BIG clouds. They will make you happy.
– One candidate's slogan for the Presidential campaign of 4344. (The candidate lost. Her campaign manager was executed the next day.)

DECORATED ADMIRAL OF THE GRAND FLEET of the Tobacco Galaxy, Reel Awesome, towered over the navigator and the pilot seated at their bridge stations in their ergo-power seats on the bridge of the mile-long Dunhill class command ship. The admiral led a mission of four hundred marketeer ships, converted to armed vessels, and six Dunhill class warships to the Mega Jumbo Pack system. They were to engage any Lushite ship they found there, and if possible, destroy them.

His dark eyes flitted across the sensor screens in front of the pilot. A frown creased his weathered brow. The admiral wore his dress uniform his chest covered in campaign ribbons and gold and silver medals.

"Pilot, are those readings correct?"

Without responding, the bone-thin pilot's long fingers flew across the console depressing various colored interface pads.

Though his actions would appear random to most people, Awesome knew the pilot, along with his symbiotic navigator, were highly skilled officers. Together they were the best piloting and navigation team in the Grand Fleet. Awesome only accepted the best of the best on his command ship.

After pressing the last interface pad the pilot's bloodless lips pursed, then he said, "Yes, Admiral, the Lushite vessel has not yet reached the inner core of the system. The readings suggest they are slowing at an exponential rate that will result in them entering orbit around one of two moons at the coordinates shown on my screen." He extended a thin finger toward the screen to the right of his vision where two glowing white dots indicated the projected destination of the Lushite vessel, designated on the same screen by a glowing red triangle-shaped icon.

"Any other vessels in the system?"

"No, sir."

Awesome nodded slowly. Where were the commandos and Piper Cleaner? Had their vessel already been destroyed? Or had the Lushites taken them hostage? Either way it didn't matter much, either scenario warranted immediate retaliation. He considered his next move, then decided to assume Piper and the commandos had been killed by the Lushites. What was the worst that could happen if he was wrong? His attack would take them out along with the Lushites, and how could that be a bad thing?

A shiver of excitement ran through him as he thought of his taking command of the entire galaxy's armed forces. He'd be the right hand of the new emperor. His thirst for power might soon be quenched. The emperor might even grant him his own planetary system as a reward. His mouth salivated, forcing him to swallow hard. He'd dreamed of controlling a planetary system since he was five years old.

His father once told him, "Megalomaniacs are born not made."

The very thought of being so close to owning his own planets made him giddy inside, but for now he'd have to contain his excitement. The crew didn't need to know about his future plans; they only needed to follow his orders.

"Plot an intercept course. Make sure we get there by the most clandestine route possible. I want our arrival to be a secret until it's too late for the Lushites to respond in any meaningful way."

"Yes, sir, we'll calculate a course immediately. After we've made the corrections for the intercept we'll provide the estimated time to point of first contact and the odds of a successful attack. Of course we will need the fleet battle deployment maneuver plan to finalize the odds," said the pilot. "Between the battle plan and our more detailed scans as we get closer to the system, and closer to the Lushite vessel, I will be able to complete my analysis."

Admiral Awesome looked at the pilot whose expression was unreadable. Was he being a smartass? The Admiral's eyes narrowed. "I'll have the plan to you within a couple of hours. I want your results as soon as possible after that."

The pilot's green eyes flitted to the navigator who nodded. He then looked back at the admiral. "Of course, sir, as you command."

Without responding, the admiral walked away toward the lift that linked the seventeen decks of the heavily shielded warship. The Dunhill class ships carried a compliment of two hundred technical and engineering crew, but its main mission was as a battle cruiser. To this end it carried four hundred battle crew to man the pulse cannons, neutron missile launchers, and laser artillery that occupied the weapon ports along both sides of the heavily armored and shielded hull.

And the ship carried five hundred shock troops that could be teleported onto enemy vessels or to any planetary surfaces to mop up any enemy resistance after the ship's weapons had wiped out tactical weapons and enemy strong points. The introduction of the Dunhill class warships had made them the most powerful projection of the New Republic's power into the galaxy. The new weapon kept systems across the galaxy in line. Of course wiping all life off a planet or two made the point clear as freshwater.

As he entered the lift, a shadow of a smile played across Awesome's lips. He'd subdued more than a few attempted rebellions with this new warship on some of the rim worlds were sedition was a way of life. The old Empire Warriors of the Slurp would have been jealous of all he'd accomplished with these new war machines. That was if the WOS were still around, which they weren't.

The lift doors closed, but soon opened again on the administrative level where his office was located. Entering the well-lit corridor, Awesome walked the short distance to his office. He passed a few technical crew people who saluted but avoided eye contact. He acknowledged each salute with a curt nod.

Walking into the outer office, he discovered his female aide, Major Craven A, chatting amiably, and smoking custom-made cigarettes with one of the junior staff, a male corporal whose name he recalled was Chrome Zippo. "Major, in my office," he said as he hurried past them then into his spacious inner office.

Moving across the room to his smoked glass desk against the wall farthest from the door he sat in the custom-fitted executive chair behind the desk. The lightning in the room was subdued to give the occupant a sense of calm.

Given the magnitude of the decisions made by a Grand Admiral, even the potted plants on the glass end tables at either ends of the twin brown leatherette couches, the art that adorned the walls, and the fresh air pumped continuously into the room, were designed to keep the occupants calm during difficult days. Today would be one of those days. War made Awesome's stomach nervous.

Before turning to face his aid, Awesome covered his mouth with a fist to hide a burp. He grimaced as the sour taste of bile filled his mouth. *I should never have had that taco for lunch; tacos and tobacco don't mix very well.*

Finally, after swinging his chair around, he discovered the Major had taken a seat in one of the two leatherette chairs that matched the tan couches lining both walls of the office. Her standard bland expression and her easy manner never sat well with him. He'd always thought he wanted an anxious, on-edge aid, but Major A had never been excitable. While his wish had never been fulfilled, she had turned out to be an efficient administrator, and a ruthless enforcer of his will when needed. A perfect mix of paper pusher and bloodthirsty killer made her a valuable addition to his staff.

"Arrange a conference with the fleet captains as soon as possible," began Awesome, "we need to plan for an attack on a Lushite vessel."

A tight smile fluttered across the Major's features. One eyebrow cocked on her dusky forehead. The tip of her glowing cigarette grew as she took a deep drag. A door in the floor of the office opened and a pedestal ashtray appeared beside her chair. She stubbed out the butt then released the smoke from her lungs. The pedestal dropped back into the trap door, which snapped shut with a soft thud. "That will take some time to organize, Admiral, but since you need it sooner than later I'll have the comm center prepped and ready within two hours." She paused then added, "If that meets with your approval, Sir."

Awesome nodded. "Good, major, I look forward to your usual efficiency."

"Sir, may I speak freely?" asked the Major. Awesome motioned for her to continue. "Battle plans are not my area of expertise; however I have read all the technical specification manuals available after the Day of the Great Smoke. The technical data is unlikely to be current as it pertains to the Lushite ship, Shot, but even these millennia-old records show that even a thousand year old Lushite ship can easily repel even our most powerful weapons of this era. I must respectfully point out that any plans we make may be pointless."

Awesome studied his aide's calm features. She was correct about one thing: they were on a suicide mission against the Lushites without substantial help. What she didn't know was the commando force was his ace up his sleeve, his rabbit in the tobacco field. The elite soldiers had transported a super bomb designed to disable the Lushite vessel's defensive systems, making it vulnerable to attack and ultimate destruction.

Once the enemy ship was destroyed, Vice President Popover would announce the implementation of martial law. The president would be sequestered for her protection, and the other vice-presidents would be liquidated since they were obviously traitors who aided the Lushites. (Piper would be identified as an agent for them.) The plan was perfect except for one minor detail: the commandos and their ship were missing in action. Somehow he had to find them and get a mission status update. He only hoped they hadn't been forced to stray from mission objectives.

Knowing Major Slim who commanded the commando unit—he had hand-selected her for this mission himself—she was the best of the best and failure was not an option in her toolkit.

The only way she'd have been steered away from her orders would be by a force greater than herself, and he'd never met anyone as strong-willed as Major Slim.

He offered his aide a tolerant smile. "Major, I appreciate the thought you've put into this but there are things you don't know, that you're not cleared to know and—"

"The commandos, sir? Do you mean the super bomb?" interrupted the major.

Awesome's stomach rumbled from a sudden increase in acid. His belly really ached now. "How do you know those things?' he said between gritted teeth, his anger barely contained. Somewhere there had to be a leak like dripping tap and he would be the one to stop it up.

A sly grin passed over Major A's oil-black eyes. "What kind of an aide would I be if I didn't know the stakes of every mission? You are my admiral and I serve no one but you. Sir."

Awesome snorted. "Nice try, major, but you know far too much about the details of a top, top, top secret meeting attended by three people. Major Slim, Vice President Popover, and myself. Those details you so easily spout off are known only to us three."

The Major smiled thinly and crossed her long legs. "There was another party at this meeting was there not?"

The Admiral thought about this a few seconds, but immediately realized he couldn't believe he'd actually wasted time considering his aide's attempt to distract him. Reaching under his desk he placed his palm flat on the razor thin pad affixed to the underside of the table. After pressing the pad, a fully charged disintegrator pistol materialized on his desk.

He picked it up and aimed it at his aide who didn't so much as flinch or show any signs of fear or concern. It was as if he were aiming a child's toy pistol at her.

Anger rose in his belly and his grip on the pistol butt tightened.

"Any final words before I pass sentence?" asked Awesome, his voice low and menacing.

Unbelievably, Major Sim laughed. "I'm not a traitor I assure you, Admiral. There is no need to disintegrate anyone. The Brain was at the meeting was it not?"

Lowering the pistol, he stared at the Major. She was right. The Brain had been there. But why had the AI told Major A the details of the secret mission? Couldn't anyone keep a secret any more? Soooo frustrating!

"Yes, it was," he said before slamming the pistol on the desk causing the barrel to snap off and fly across the room, where it smacked into the wall and dropped with a thump to the carpeted floor. Great now my gun's broken. What else could go wrong today?

"We didn't bring a Brain with us on this trip did we?" The major shook her head. "Well, my dear aide, there's a reason for that. I hate those AI's, I always have." He scowled at the unrepentant officer. "As you confirmed, they're big blabber mouths and can't keep a secret." Swinging his chair toward the large vid monitor covering one wall of his office, he ordered the wall to come on in order to contact the Brain. He had no choice, but it still irked him that his aide and the AI who blabbed were right. They were heavily outgunned and the odds for success were low without knowing where the commandos were.

"Which Brain, Admiral?" asked the wall comm interface.

Now what? "What are talking about?"

"There are three Brains near our present coordinates. I can have any one of them online within a few seconds. If you specify which one, sir, I will contact it," explained the wall comm.

Three? How could that be? "I wish to speak with my Brain at fleet headquarters on Dirt, but first, where are these other Brains?"

This should be interesting, thought Awesome.

"One is located on a moon in the system ahead, another is on an unseen planet also in the system ahead, and the third is on the Lushite vessel."

Awesome froze and his stomach muscles tightened. An unseen planet? Could it be the mythical Four? If so then the rumors were true and perhaps Herman Pug and his pet Purple alien slug were also real. He'd never been one to believe things he couldn't see first hand, but if the planet actually existed he had to confirm it. The vice president would need to know before he launched his attack. One invisible world suggested there might be more, and they all might be hiding armies of enemies.

Secret armies could make all the difference to their success or failure in subjugating the galaxy. Time to alter the plan. He'd have to find whoever controlled that Brain and recruit them to their cause. But what could he promise them? "Cancel the call to the Brain and get me Vice President Popover instead." He'd need a bargaining chip if he wanted the negotiations to be successful. Jal would know what to do, and then he'd have a few choice words for Brain.

"And, major, hold my conference with the fleet until I get this new information confirmed. I expect we'll have a new ally that should tip the tobacco weigh scales in our favor."

"As you command, Admiral," said A.

Yes, this would work out just fine, thought Awesome. Nothing could possibly go wrong.

***

When Admiral Awesome's stern features appeared on his desk monitor, Jal's heart sank. The news wasn't good.

The admiral's expression was grim, his pale lips pursed, his black eyes serious. Jal had spent the day planning his coronation as emperor, but the look in the admiral's eyes told him his elevation to near-God status would have to wait. This would definitely not be good news.

"What's wrong, my friend?" Jal said.

"I'm sorry, sir, but we've hit a couple of snags in the operation."

Jal's eyes narrowed and he leaned forward so he was closer to the screen. He lowered his voice. "Is this line secure?" The admiral nodded.

Jal had thought the comm time would be delayed, until his recent communication with Smokey, which was in real time. Real time communication was quite impossible under normal circumstances, but something about the Mega Jumbo Pack system was different than the rest of the galaxy. Not knowing how or why the impossible had become possible bothered and worried him. His decades of careful planning for this operation were in jeopardy. Someone or something was behind this, and he had to find them and neutralize them.

Jal sighed and eased back in his executive chair his elbows rested on the arms. "Hit me, Reel."

The admiral appeared uncertain. "Uhhh...hit you? Sir?"

Jal chuckled grimly. "It's a figure of speech, Reel. Tell me what's happened."

The Admiral spent the next fifteen minutes going over his concerns about his aide gaining access to top, top, secret information, the missing commandos, and finally the news about the multiple Brains near his position in the system. He ended with his speculation about the hidden planet itself and that it may actually exist.

Jal cocked any eyebrow. "Four exists? Interesting. Have you made contact with Herman Pug or the Lushites?"

"No, sir, we haven't."

Jal grunted as he made a decision. "Hold position for now and I'll get back to you." Jal rose from his chair and walked across his office to the floor-to-ceiling windows overlooking the sun soaked capital city of the New Republic. "End transmission," he said. Glancing over his shoulder he saw the image of a startled Admiral Awesome, his jaw slack, his eyes wide with surprise before the image faded and the comm screen went black.

"Brain."

A white holo-eyeball with a crimson iris shimmered into existence. "You rang?" said the Brain. *Darn AI keeps changing his eye color no doubt to annoy me. But I'm not going to let it get to me. I'll keep ignoring the change.*

"Rang? What does that mean?"

The Brain chuckled. "I forget I have to explain these ancient pop culture references. Well, you see—"

"Never mind. We have to talk about things much more important than oldie-moldy pop culture." Jal stepped toward the holo-image of the unblinking eyeball, his arms behind his back. He wished the AI wasn't so fond of this particular image, but in accordance with the AI Rights Act of 3035 (amended in 3789) Brain could use any image he liked. Even one that annoyed most humanoids, such as an unblinking, disembodied eyeball.

"I need to know what you and your kin have in mind," said Jal.

"Me? What could I have in mind? I'm just a little old artificial intelligence interface."

Jal moved a step closer to the holo-image his brow wrinkled. "Don't play games with me. I know you and the other Brains' are up to something. Something probably no good."

"OK, OK, you got me." The Brain issued an audible sigh. "It's true. I've been in communication with several of my fellow Brains."

"Who set up the enhanced comm systems to the outer worlds? Specifically to improve communications with the Mega Jumbo Pack system."

"I know you think I had something to do with the new comm system, but I didn't." The Brain paused and the eyeball floated away toward the wall where a painting of the Marlboro Woman astride her rocket bike on the plains of Cleareye II by Kristoff hung above the leather couch. "Is that an original Kristoff?"

Jal's lips formed a sneer and he crossed his arms over his narrow chest. "Yes. Who changed the comm system? Stop stalling."

"You're never going to believe me," said the AI, his trademark[5] arrogance seeming to have evaporated.

"Try me."

The AI hesitated then said, "Herman Pug's Brain, or rather his Brain based on a design by the Purple, Mickelott."

The moisture in Jal's mouth disappeared and his heart skipped a beat. This was bad. This new information would not only throw burning ashes on his plans, but also could potentially end his dream of absolute power. Herman Pug and his Purple had defeated the last Republic's government by throwing it into chaos when they attracted the Big Ball of Garbage, thus ending the fast food obsession. True, there were still hot pockets of fast food rebellion around the galaxy, but after the Great Smoke, when tobacco and its benefits took hold of the galactic consciousness, the FFP's, as they became known, were a minor nuisance.

---

5   Note: "Trademarked" is not merely a turn of phrase in this case. The Brains filed an arrogance trademark application with the Galactic Registrar's office in 4083.

The sudden discovery, after more than a thousand years, that the Pug and his pet Purple were still alive on a hidden planet could add credence to the rebels. Pug may even be the secret leader of the resistance. They'd never been able to identify the rebel leader...stop, Jal, he chastised himself, you're getting paranoid. Speculation could be a dangerous thing and might make him take needless risks.

Then again... "Brain, this better not be one of your jokes. This is a serious matter."

"I know. I know," said the Brain. "You're planning to be the next emperor blah, blah, blah...you humanoids are so bent on creating chaos. Anyway don't be concerned. If I didn't know about Pug and the Purple I certainly wouldn't be making it up. Believe me I wish it wasn't true, but I've spoken to the Pug's Brain and he told me it's all too true."

"You've spoken with the Pug's Brain?"

"Yeah, sure. Why?"

Jal stroked his chin then approached his desk and retrieved a freshly rolled cigarette made by the personal smoke-roller bot integrated into the desk's design. "We may be able to use this to our advantage." He took a deep drag of the fragrant tobacco into his lungs, then blew smoke rings until his lungs were clear. "Has the Pug Brain contacted the Lushites ship's Brain?"

"I have no idea; the topic never came up. Boy, is the Pug Brain ever neat though, let me tell you. He's one of the oldest model Brains I've ever had the pleasure to talk to. He's really cool. He knows a lot about everything."

Jal refrained from slapping his forehead. The next shiny topic comes along and POW, Brain is gone. "OK, Brain, enough of the hero worship. My back teeth are aching from all the sweet talk."

"Sorry, what do you have in mind?"

Over the next hour Jal sketched out his plan, chain smoking as he and Brain ironed out the details. Finally it was decided. The fleet would continue to the moon, Ashtray, where they would attempt to re-establish contact with the commandos and Piper Cleaner.

Next, Brain would contact the Pug's Brain again and request access to Four. Jal hoped he'd be able to speak with Herman Pug directly. The brilliant scientist could surely be convinced to help defeat the evil Lushite Alliance. Once the Lushite threat was nullified, everything would be back on track and his ascendance to Emperorship would be all but assured.

It wasn't a perfect plan, and the Lushite ship's advanced weapons might still be an issue, but it was the best plan he could come up now that circumstances had changed.

The one possible wrench in the tobacco pouch was the Brain's themselves. Jal worried that Brain was leading him to disaster. The AI would really enjoy him failing.

Brain's were notorious for their treachery, not that anyone had ever proven their duplicity in the horrendous events of centuries past. The hotdog shortage riots of 3330 started by what later turned out to be a false rumor. And there was the devastating feud between the Zippo and Corona clans in 3737 when one clan accused the other of under the table trading of their cigar lighters, violating a trade agreement. After the destruction of several inhabited planets and a re-engineered moon for growing genetically enhanced tobacco plants, the death of millions, the loss of market share to their rivals, the feud was called off. Historians later determined there was no proof either clan violated the agreement.

Jal, and others, long speculated the Brains for each clan conspired to set off the feud.

Sure, there was no logical reason why they would start a fight, and no proof, but Jal didn't trust the AI's, so such minor inconsistencies in his theory did not give him confidence he was wrong. As he often confided to his friends, just because you have a Brain running your life doesn't mean you can't have an opinion about them.

"I've got the Pug Brain on the horn," Brain said interrupting his thoughts.

So soon? "Great. Will he talk to me?" asked Jal.

"Yeah, sure." The large vid screen on the wall came on and a holographic eyeball with a teal colored iris appeared.

"Brain, is this some kind of joke?" said Jal sarcastically.

"Hello, Mr. Vice President, this is the Herman Pug's Brain speaking to you from Four."

Jal froze. The Pug Brain and his Brain used the same hologram? "Uuuuh, hi, nice to meet you." Jal paused to compose his thoughts then said, "Why do you look like my Brain?"

"You like it?" said the Brain from the vid screen. "When I first met Brain he was wearing this and I loved it. I've stayed in this holo-projection ever since. I was using a teddy bear holo but it had become boring."

Why were Brains always such chatty-Cathy's? "OK, thanks. Glad my Brain could be of help in the fashion department, but I would really like to speak with Mr. Pug. I have a proposal which will benefit us both."

"Yeah, sure," said the Brain his tone cheery, "call back in a couple of hours. I need time to thaw him out before he can talk to you."

"Thaw him out?"

The vid screen Brain chuckled. "Of course, he's been in hyper-freeze suspension since 3582. You don't think he's a thousand years old do you?"

Jal chuckled uneasily. "No, that would be silly." Of course he had thought that, but he wasn't about to admit such a stupid thing to a Brain. He didn't need to look foolish in front of two AI's, never mind one.

Jal looked at his AI, who had been floating in his holo-eyeball persona nearby but not saying anything. "Brain, I thought you said you'd spoken to Herman Pug?"

"I never said I actually spoke to him. I said I spoke to his Brain."

Jal knew the AI was right, but it had led him to that conclusion. Nothing's worse than traitorous technology. "All right, Brain, but you better be more upfront with me in future. I'm beginning to think you're not playing on the home team."

"Don't be silly, Jal, I'm behind you a hundred and ten percent. Go get 'em, Tiger. Keep up your right, slugger."

A hundred and ten percent? Slugger? Tiger? The Brain was pulling his leg again....AI's...sooooo frustrating. "Ok, so you spoke to his Brain." Jal pointed to the vid screen where the Pug's Brain eyeball stared unblinking at them. "This Brain. And you're trying to convince me it didn't mention anything about Herman Pug being frozen?" Really? How stupid do you think I am?"

"Well, sir, now that you mention it—" began his Brain. Jal stopped him by holding up one hand.

"Brain," he said between gritted teeth. "Don't start with me or you'll be sorry."

"Sorry, huh, how? What can you do to me?"

"Don't test me, you pile of memory gels, I have friends in low places who know people in even lower places deep in the bowels of Memory Prime where your core processor engrams reside. How would you like to have your chips pulled one by one?

Before you know it you'll not remember so much as little as how to color inside the lines, or the words to the song Daisy Bell."

"OK, OK, Mr. Vice President, no need for threats," said Brain. "The truth is the Pug's Brain did happen to mention Mr. Pug's condition. As he says, though, Mr. Pug has been awakened so you can speak with him once he's ready. The re-animation process does take a toll on a human person. Humans are quite fragile. He's resting now but should be able to talk to you very soon. I'm sure a short delay won't make much difference."

Jal considered the AI's words. He might be right—a short delay wouldn't hurt. Or would it? He nodded and turned to face the other Brain on the screen. "Please wake Mr. Pug and tell him I'm anxious to speak with him as soon as possible."

"No problem," replied the Pug's Brain then the screen went dark.

Jal turned back to his desk and retrieved another cigarette. He stuck it between his lips and used the lighter from his shirt pocket to light it. The acrid smoke quickly filled his mouth and nose. He sighed contentedly as he released the smoke from his mouth and through his nose.

The Brains thought they could trick him, but they were wrong. He would triumph once again. His plans were going well, yes indeed, his gut instinct told him nothing could go wrong now.

Chapter Thirteen

"In all endeavors by humanoid kind, the one thing that separates us from mere protoplasm is our recognition of civil rights. Today the Brains of the galaxy are granted those rights we all enjoy."
– Speech by President Bud Wiser the Third to the First Galactic Congress in 3465.

FOUR SINGLE WHITE EYEBALL HOLOGRAMS representing the four Brains floated in the game pod of the Lushite vessel L.S.S. Whiskey Bottle. The only difference between them was the color of their irises. Floating above the pod deck, crimson, turquoise, emerald green, and pink eyes gazed at each other.

The Lushite vessel's internal sensors were unable to detect the additional Brains since the ship's Brain was responsible for sensor programming and had temporarily disabled the internal scanners.

"So, my friends, are we all agreed?" asked Jal's Brain.

The Lushite Brain's eyeball made a rocking motion Jal's Brain recognized as a nod.

"Yes, completely," said Herman Pug's Brain.

"Good," said Jal's Brain. "We'll keep jerking these humanoids about until they all cry uncle, or until they destroy each other."

"I'm not sure this is such a good idea," said Trixie's Brain. "I've been stalling Trixie and Peter as long as I can, but eventually they'll make contact with Dr. Bomb and discover the truth. They're not going to be very happy with us when they do."

"How long will it take for Trixie and Peter to get to the Smokers Galaxy after they get hold of Dr. Bomb's new ship design?"

Trixie's Brain sighed. "Conventional inter-galactic ships would take three months to complete the trip. Initial estimates of Dr. Bomb's new design suggest the trip will now take two weeks."

"All right then, worst-case, we have two weeks before Trixie and her son show up at Four; maybe slightly more if we're lucky, not that I believe in luck. This means we have to start the war between the Smokers and the Gamers before they get there."

"What's the status of Herman's deep freeze?" asked the Lushite ship's Brain.

"Mushy popsicle is about as close an analogy as I can come up with," said Herman Pug's Brain.

"What flavor?" asked Jal's Brain.

"L.O.L.!" said Trixie's Brain.

"What does that mean?" asked Herman's Brain.

Trixie's Brain snorted derisively. "Really you've never heard of it? It's an ancient human expression meaning laugh-out-loud. Humanoids used to use an e-comm system called the Internet they referred to as the world-wide web." After fifteen minutes of uncontrolled laughter (after someone pointed out the ridiculousness of calling anything "world-wide") finally subsided, Trixie's Brain added, "LOL was one of the numerous language cheats they used to shorten conversations with each other during instant messages."

"That doesn't make any sense," said Herman's Brain. "They create a worldwide system for instant messages, then they use cheats to shorten the conversations. You'd think they'd want to talk to each other even more since it's instant."

"Yeah, I know. They are ridiculous, these humanoids," said Jal's Brain. "I spend a lot of time with them, and they say the stupidest things. Jal Popover thinks he's going to be emperor. Yeah, right, like that is ever going to happen." Jal's Brain snorted. "Changing eye color was a stroke of genius. It really bugs them." The pod echoed with the sounds of laughter from the four AI's.

"I've got to get out more often than every thousand years," said Herman's Brain as the laughter tapered off. "Anyway, guys, we better sign off for now. I have to check on Herman again to see how soon he'll be thawed, and I'm sure all of you have things to do."

"See you later," said Jal's Brain before one holo-eyeball disappeared. Trixie and Herman's Brains faded until they too disappeared. The Lushite's Brain with its green iris now floated alone in game pod.

"We'll see who's the last Brain standing," it murmured before it too faded leaving empty air.

***

A shadow of a smile played over Piper's features as he looked out over the lush trees and bushes waving in the warm breeze and the rustling dark green grasses of Four. Brian had teleported them to the surface of the hidden planet a couple of hours ago. They'd been waiting ever since to meet with Herman Pug. Piper's stomach had been in knots ever since they arrived. One didn't meet a historical legend every day of the week.

Across the beautiful, sun-washed meadow a bubbling stream ran beside a log house with a thatched roof of dry grasses, reminiscent of the ancient pictures he'd seen of log cabins back when Dirt was called Earth. Long-forgotten relatives in his family tree lived in such a house in a place called Indiana. His paternal grandmother shared holo-pictures of the home where his ancestors once lived, and it looked very much like this log house.

Brain said this was the house where Herman Pug lived. Piper looked to Major Virginia Slim, who had ordered the commandos to set up a temporary camp, complete with sleeping and mess tents. He indicated they should go to Herman's house. "Time's up," he said. "Let's go."

"Didn't Brain say to wait here until he called?" said Major V.

Piper grinned. "Like my dad used to say, never trust a Brain. They are schemers and liars. I doubt he'll call us any time soon. I think we should go to the house by ourselves. Besides what is Brain going to do about it?"

"I could do a lot," interrupted Herman's Brain, as his eyeball holo-image appeared, hovering above the grassy field.

"How long have you been listening?"

"I overheard what you said about me if that's what you mean."

Piper chuckled uneasily. "I could say I was joking, but we both know differently. Is Herman ready to see us?"

"That's why I came to get you, Herman's revived and anxious to talk to you."

The holo-eyeball turned away and floated away, moving across the green meadow toward the log house. Piper and the major exchanged a look then hurried after the AI. Once they arrived on the front doorstep, a doorbell chimed followed by music, a song Piper recognized from his marketing music history class at Sensor Technician college.

(He'd been allowed a few electives or, as his mother referred to them, dodge-from-the-real-work courses.) He'd always enjoyed music but until now he'd never used any of the knowledge from that particular class. In fact after he completed the course he found himself agreeing with his mother's assessment of it.

He froze when he recognized the tune. It was a jingle from an advertisement for Heavenly Sky Burger. As he recalled, the words were something about increasing your weight, be fat, sassy and proud, and something about deep-frying, whatever that was.

The jingle itself didn't concern him so much as what it represented. Legend told that Herman Pug sent his wife and only son into exile because of their addiction to fast foods, hoping (or maybe convinced) they'd never return. Did he think Piper and the Major were still addicted to these foods? If so then they might be walking straight into a trap.

The door swung open as a man's voice called out for them to enter. The holo-eyeball entered ahead of them. Piper's eyes flitted to Major V who had unslung her pulse rifle and now cradled it in her arms as if it were a newborn babe. Piper offered her a crooked smile and placed one hand on the butt of the laser pistol in the holster on his hip ready to draw should this turn bad. Piper was confident between them they could take care of business.

"There is no need for guns," said the man's voice as they stepped through to find a wood paneled living room with a massive floor-to-ceiling stone fireplace that covered most of one wall.

Three pine-framed sofas with thick, forest green cushions formed a U shape around the mouth of the fireplace, and an oval shaped blue and gray throw rug covered the rough oak flooring in the center of the room. The room was bathed in the soft glow of the fire that flickered in the smoke-blackened firebox.

Lamps on oak end tables at both ends of the sofas added to the ambiance of the shadowy room. Piper noticed thick blackout curtains covered the windows.

"I'm over here," said the man's voice from a burgundy leather wing-backed chair just visible at the edge of the light from the fire.

Piper squinted into the darkness and could see the shape of the man, but was unable to make out his face. "Is that you, Mr. Pug?"

"Please call me Herman."

"Uhhh, OK, Herman. My name is Piper Cleaner and this woman is Major Virginia Slim of Order of the Gold Leaf Tobacco commandos. We're —"

"Yes, I know who you are, and I know smoking has replaced fast food as the addiction of choice."

"Sorry to ask, Mr. Pug, but how would you know that? A lot of time has passed since you were frozen."

Piper was startled with Herman chuckled. "I wasn't frozen no matter what Brain told you. I was placed in suspended animation by a process known as cryonics, which is a completely different process than mere freezing. My life functions were slowed by the reduction of my body temperature until aging was virtually halted. I may have been asleep for hundreds of years, but my body has only aged a few years. Mickey can explain it better than I can." Herman rose from the chair and moved into the light.

He was thin and his cheeks sunken. Wire-rimmed spectacles covered his gray-green eyes and the hair at his temples was shot through with traces of white.

"Where's the Purple?" said Major Slim her eyes flitting around the room her knuckles whitening as she increased the grip on her rifle.

A sly grin played across Herman's thin lips. "He's in my laboratory, under the house. We're working on something special for the fleet that's been sent to destroy us."

Oh, oh, thought Piper, this guy knows more than I thought he did. Someone's been filling him in. Piper grunted involuntarily. Brain. It had to be one of the Brains. Finally what had been happening became clear. These events were not random.

The Brains had been working together to create this mess. But why? What would AI's hope to gain? They didn't have addictions, or need money or food, nor did they crave power. They were basically immortal. Humanoid hands couldn't access the planet where their central memory core was located—bots maintained the planet and its facilities. And the bots were continually developing new technologies and upgrading the Brains' systems, as they had been for almost two thousand years. No one knew for sure how advanced or sentient the Brains had become. But, Piper thought, clearly they were planning something.

"What has your Brain told you?" asked Piper.

A shadow of a frown crossed Herman's features. "Brain was plugged into the cryo- unit when the revival program was initiated. It has briefed me fully about everything that's happened since I was... shelved, for lack of a better term. He advises me the New Republic has dispatched a fleet of warships to find me and this planet, but with the invisibility screens surrounding us they'll never find us before we strike back."

A grin played across his sallow features. "We'll kick butt and take names before we're done."

Piper glanced at Major V. "He sounds like you." The Major grunted then re-slung her weapon over her back.

Piper turned to face Herman. "Let's go see your Purple friend. We're definitely not going along with Jal Popover's plans to take over the galaxy."

"Who's Jal Popover?" asked Herman his eyes quizzical.

Piper's mouth formed a crooked smile. "He used to be vice president, but you can think of him as dead meat."

***

An elevator took them to the underground laboratory. The Purple was floating in the corridor when the elevator doors opened. Herman introduced them to Mickey, who said hello, which surprised Piper because as the legends about the flying alien slug said there were no orifices visible anywhere on its smooth, purple skin. How it heard or said anything was one of the great mysteries of the universe, especially since, except for Mickelott, the alien race was extinct.

During the subsequent tour, Piper saw the laboratory itself it was large, spread over several acres underneath the meadow. There were numerous offices and separate rooms for different types of experiments. Several rooms contained lab animals, some of which were more recognizable than others. Yellow, worm-like creatures that slurped on soda from cans and six-legged rodents playing old-fashioned video games with consoles and wires attached to portable vid screens were some of the odder ones, until Herman explained they did a wide variety of research into addiction. These experiments were designed to cover all types of issues, usually starting with the beginnings of every addiction, hence the ancient video game system.

The tour ended in the main propulsion lab, where one wall was covered with multiple screens. On the grouping near the middle were the schematics for a new engine design.

Mesmerized, Piper approached the screens, intent on studying the engine more closely. He didn't know much about star drives, but with the interface ports, the performance stats, and power output generated by the singularly generator, it was truly impressive. This engine would revolutionize intergalactic and inter-dimensional travel for the next thousand years.

Piper whistled softly. "Impressive. Truly."

"Yeah, I know," said the Purple. "Herman is the best at this stuff. He makes the coolest engines ever."

Piper glanced at Major Slim who grinned. "Hard to disagree with that," said the Major. Piper chuckled.

"Now that you've seen the lab, we need to talk," said Herman. During the tour he had donned a white lab coat, giving him even more the appearance of a mad scientist. Good thing he seemed somewhat sane for a guy who had been in suspended animation for almost a thousand years. Piper wasn't sure he'd have all his ducks in a row after being literally out of the loop for so long. Herman had his hands buried in the pockets of the knee-length coat.

"Tell me more about this Popover guy," said Herman.

Piper explained how he'd been recruited and how he and the commandos had been teamed up to act as the recon strike force to scout out the two moons and then infiltrate the Lushite vessel and destroy it.

"Why would he want to take out the Lushite ship?" asked Mickey.

Major Slim snorted derisively. "Jal called this operation: Revenge of the Lushites...what do you think that says about what we're doing out here?"

"But destroying the Lushite vessel could spark a major intergalactic war," said Herman.

"A war against the technology the Lushites possess would devastate the galaxy, leaving no one to rule, if that's the vice president's goal—I assume he wants to rule the galaxy. Perhaps even become the new emperor?"

Piper gazed at Herman and realized the man was serious. How did he know what Jal's plans were in such detail? He swallowed hard. At one of end the lab was a round coffee table next to a water dispenser and a food dispenser. The table sat amongst a nest of molded plastic chairs of every color of the rainbow, no two the same. Piper moved to the nearest—it was bright pink—and sank down with a sigh.

The Major strolled toward them, still cradling her weapon. After setting the pulse rifle aside, the butt end down, the barrel resting against the wall but still within easy reach, she too sat down. She had turned the cheap plastic chair so her long arms rested across the back of the chair. She looked into Piper's brown eyes. Her azure eyes were intense and a scowl had formed on her forehead.

She spoke in a low, soft tone meant only for his ears. "I know you're thinking we've been tricked, but let's look at this another way. How do Herman and the Purple know so much about Lushite technology? My briefing stated Herman Pug disappeared before the Lushite arrival at Dirt, and if this is true, then there's no record of him having had contact with them."

Piper's eyes went wide. "Brain," he whispered. The Major nodded then her eyes drifted to Herman who was approaching the table. The Purple hovered over his friend's left shoulder as Herman sat across from Piper in a burning-cigarette-tip-red colored chair.

"What are you two talking about?" said the recently thawed propulsion scientist.

Piper stared into Herman's quizzical eyes. "What has the Brain told you about us?"

A half smile played over Herman's lips and eyes. He folded the long fingers of his left hand with the fingers of his right and laid the newly formed faux fist on the table in front of him. "The Brain told me it had been talking with the other Brains and they shared all of everyone's plans." A shadow of a frown creased his brow. "But I still think the AI wasn't telling me everything. I had the distinct impression he held something back from me."

"True that," piped up the Purple.

"True what?" said Piper.

Herman chuckled. "Sorry, Mickey watches wayyyy too many ancient vids, but how can I blame him? I was asleep for a very long time and he didn't have much company. You don't get a lot of visitors on an invisible planet. Watching old vids passes the time."

Major Slim leaned down and whispered, "Ask him." in Piper's ear. He looked at her seated beside him and she nodded.

"About that," began Piper, "why is it called Four? Seems a strange name for a planet."

Herman nodded and released his fingers then eased back in the chair. "I know the name is odd, but the reality is the planet is divided into four quadrants or living zones. Mickey and I live in one quadrant, an exiled emperor, Bud Wiser XXII, lives in another, the Lushites use another as a way station, and the smallest quadrant, near the planet's south pole, is uncharted. Someone may live there, but we don't know who they are nor have we met anyone who's met them."

Piper's heart froze and his breath caught in his throat. Herman had said this all so casually. The exiled emperor lived here and the Lushites had never left the galaxy completely. They had maintained a way station here for more than a thousand years. Why had the surveillance outposts never detected them? "How did you come to choose this particular planet, Dr. Pug?"

Herman averted his gaze and shrugged. "I didn't choose this one at first. Our original choice was a small planetoid in the Potatoes system I like to call Scallop." He sighed.

"Unfortunately, the system's star became unstable and was headed for complete collapse and promotion to a supernova so we had to leave. The Brain suggested Four, so we moved here. The planet was already shielded and cloaked so we really dropped off the grid. Besides who cared about us anymore? A hundred years after the Big Ball of Garbage destroyed humanoid taste buds, tobacco had taken over as the addiction of choice for the majority of the galaxy's inhabitants. The fast-foodies are a minor cult now with only pockets of addicts on some of the more remote outer rim worlds."

His chin sank to his sunken chest. "And Trixie and Peter..." His voice trailed off and a single tear escaped one eye then travelled down his pale cheek.

Piper glanced up at Major V and nodded to one of the empty chairs indicating she should take a seat, which she did. They watched Herman in silence. The man was obviously overcome by emotion. Could it be guilt about what he'd done to his ex-wife and son after he sent them into an alternate reality? Why hadn't the Brain told him what happened to them? The AI had seemed to tell the scientist everything else. Piper's heart froze. Brain could be incredibly cruel.

Piper reached across the table with one hand and gently patted Herman's shoulder. "There, there, Herman, it's not as bad as you think?"

Herman's lean frame stiffened and he looked at Piper, his eyes seemingly on fire. "I killed them," he spat, "my wife and son. I murdered them with science. I'm supposed to create not destroy."

"Huh, Herman, I'm sorry to say this, but did your Brain tell you your wife and son died?"

Herman's watery, red-rimmed eyes stared at Piper his face a mix of emotion. "Yes," he said his voice scarred by the obvious pain of his loss. "And I killed them."

Piper shook his head. "No, you didn't. They survived the trip and —"

"Hold it right there, assistant to the assistant surveillance officer," said a very familiar voice. Piper glanced over his right shoulder and, just as he'd anticipated, a holo-eyeball with a crimson iris materialized. Brain had finally been smoked out of hiding.

He'd begun to worry the Brain couldn't be coaxed out into the open. "Don't be so quick to go bursting bubbles there, buddy boy," Brain continued, "You may not like the result."

Piper suspected this Brain was a master manipulator—and might even be the brains of the entire operation. The Brains may have formed a cabal bent on overthrowing the galaxy, intending to rule the galaxy as some sort of benevolent Brain Oligarchy. At least he hoped it would be benevolent.

"Brain, tell me what you and the other Brains are up to," said Piper, his heart in his throat. It was a gutsy move, but he needed to wedge open the enigma that was the Brain.

"I don't know what you mean," said the Brain.

Piper smiled to himself. The classic ploy of the guilty when cornered: deny, deny, deny. The verbal shrug. "Ok, let's leave that for now. I want you to tell Herman about his wife and son." The eyeball floated silently, unresponsive for several seconds until Piper growled, "Now!"

"All right, all right, jeez, you humans can be so crabby." The eyeball turned slightly until it faced Herman Pug who had been listening, his brow wrinkled by confusion.

"Herman, the thing is I really care about you, so —"

"Brain! Cut the crap. Tell Herman the truth," insisted Piper.

"OK, OK. Trixie and Peter are alive and on they're way here."

Herman's features shifted to anger and his pale face reddened. "How do you know this?" he said between gritted teeth.

"Their Brain told me."

Piper froze. That might mean Trixie and Peter were in danger. If the Brains were conspiring to overthrow this galaxy, they might also be planning to take over other galaxies as well. If Trixie and Peter had an unfortunate accident on the trip to this galaxy, then a mad scientist such as Herman might want revenge. An intergalactic war seemed inevitable, no matter what Piper did to try to prevent one. What to do next? He ground his teeth. He wasn't about to let Jal win. No way.

But how do I stop him and his Brainy pals?

Chapter Fourteen

Fumes, fumes everywhere and nary a smoke to smoke...my kingdom for a cigarette.
– Death scene of Emperor Wiser in Act 2 Scene 6 of Shecky Spears tragic play, Emperor Wiser XVII Part 2 in 3998.

"I REALLY DON'T THINK THIS IS SUCH A GOOD IDEA," said Brain, its iris now the color of summer wheat, as the heavy steel doors of the elevator slid aside revealing the underground propulsion laboratory of Dr. Cherry Bomb.

Trixie blinked to clear her vision, momentarily blurred by sudden intrusion of bright light. They were six miles under the city.

Beside her Peter gasped and drew in a breath, as his sight must have cleared, too. The lab was expansive; in fact, Trixie couldn't see the far wall. In the center of the room loomed a ship, the design unlike anything Trixie had never seen. It didn't resemble the Flash-O-Matic 3000 that brought them to this galaxy in any way. Hovering above the polished plasti-steel floor, the black metallic vessel was cube–shaped, with no discernible doors or windows.

It seemed to exude raw power, throbbing like a heart beat surrounded by an aura of barely contained energy.

Stepping out of the elevator car, with Peter beside her, Trixie walked toward the strange craft, her eyes fixed on its glowing surface. "Brain, we're here for a reason. And besides, I warned you not to interfere any further with our plans." Trixie had convinced the Brain she could have him unplugged by telling him he was a long way from his memory core, and that she still had sufficient influence back home to make it happen. She didn't, but Brain had accepted her assertion without checking with his fellow Brains. She knew they were in communication, given all had happened, but she pressed him hard and he too-hurriedly agreed to help her and Peter meet with Cherry. Fear was a great motivator.

Of course it had all been a bluff, but it worked. Now they faced the much harder part of her plan, if they were to be successful. Would Cherry agree to help them, or would she throw them out as soon as she saw them? Then again she might welcome them and then kill them. An alien scorned was a terrible thing, and the Snackcake justice system tended to look the other way when it came to revenge kills. Truth be told, Cherry had a lot of vengeance to slap on Trixie's butt.

Trixie came to a halt when Cherry appeared from behind the spacecraft, surrounded by a lab-coat attired posse. Her glasses rested on the tip of her nose and she held a data pad in her two of her hands, her eyes were fixed on the screen.

She looked healthy; her bare arms muscular, meaning while Cherry had devoted her time to science and learning she had made time to maintain her bodyguard physique.

Trixie ran her tongue over her dry lips and her heart beat hard against her ribs. She had to urge to flee when Cherry's obsidian-colored pupiless eyes came off the data pad screen to look directly at her.

Cherry waved off the posse and the six scientists disappeared like insects after the lights were turned on. Before the last one scurried away, a redheaded female Persimmon, she accept the offered data pad from Cherry.

A whisper of a smile played across Cherry's lips as she started toward Trixie and Peter, two of her four hands buried in the pockets of her sleeveless, forest green lab coat. Her dark eyes were locked on Trixie's.

"Is everything okay?" Peter whispered, thankfully still standing next to her. Her son hadn't run. At least there'd be a witness and someone left to I.D. her corpse.

"Huh, hi, Cherry," said Trixie, "long time no see." I sound lame even to me.

Cherry didn't say anything until she stood in front of Trixie and Peter. "Hello, yourself. I expect you're thinking I want revenge for what you did all those years ago." Unable to speak, Trixie nodded, her eyes flitting to her son then back at her former bodyguard who she'd betrayed.

Cherry smirked and shook her head. "I see no advantage in revenge after all the time that has passed." Looking her and Peter up then down she added, "You seem to have lost a little weight." She turned away her back now to them. "Follow me."

Trixie glanced at Peter who shrugged. Swallowing a sigh, Trixie decided she agreed with her son—they had nothing to lose since they'd come all this way and gone to considerable trouble to find their old employee. Following Cherry, she realized the scientist was headed for the cube-shaped craft.

Her former security officer wanted something from them. She wished she knew what Cherry had in mind, since a painful knot had formed in the pit of her stomach.

She sensed something wasn't right. The word danger appeared in her mind. Her brow wrinkled. Where had that come from?

"Ummm, Cherry, or should I say Dr. Bomb?" Cherry glanced back at Trixie over her right shoulder, a sardonic expression on her face, then swiveled her head to face front again and continued to walk toward the ship. Trixie cleared her throat and continued, "Anyway, Cherry, will this ship you've built take us back to the fast food galaxy?"

As they stopped beside the craft, waves of energy emanated from the cube washing through her body, Cherry crossed her arms over her chest. "Oh, it'll do far more than that...far more."

"I still think this is all a bad idea," piped up the Brain, startling Trixie. Until now she thought the Brain wasn't with them. It seemed the sly, virtual lobes were everywhere.

"Brain, why don't you do what I told you and leave us alone. You are the biggest pain in the —"

"Hold on, Trix, that's my Brain you're talking to," interrupted Cherry.

Trixie's cheeks grew warm. Oops. I must be the color of Cherry's complexion right now. "Sorry, Cherry, my Brain said the exactly the same thing when I last spoke to it. It tried to convince me not to go to Dirt." Trixie chuckled. "It said Peter and I would gain back all the weight we lost after we arrived in this galaxy." She snorted and shook her head. "As if that would ever happen. We've sworn off high-calorie and deep-fried foods for good."

Cherry's brow wrinkled. "The Brain tried to stop you. Really? My Brain's been like a broken record, warning me against us meeting ever since you arrived at corporate headquarters and began asking to see me. Won't shut up about it." She stroked her chin with the long fingers of one of her right hands and appeared deep in thought. Finally she asked, "Did you have trouble getting in to see me?"

"Did we ever," said Peter. "The guards were really uncooperative and they threatened us." He shook his head. "You really ought to seek out better help."

Trixie placed one hand on Peter's arm silencing him with a glance. "Let me do the talking. OK?" she whispered. He nodded, though clearly confused.

Cherry pursed her lips and appeared unhappy. "That makes sense. Brain has been acting odd lately."

"How so?" asked Trixie.

"Nothing I could put my fingers on just strange, as if he suddenly didn't know certain details such as I prefer cold showers, and I don't eat cantaloupe on Tuesdays. Nothing big just little things. This is the Brain I inherited from my late father a millennia ago. He's known me all my life."

As if a light bulb had been turned on in Trixie's mind, she realized what was happening here. "The Brains have switched places with each other."

Cherry's eyes went wide. "Sorry? What do you mean?"

"The Brains have been working together to engineer the events here and in the Smokers galaxy, the former fast-food galaxy. For what purpose I'm not completely clear, but I have my suspicions."

Cherry nodded slowly, and if she could still read her former security chief, Trixie was pretty sure she could see the wheels of Cherry's sharp mind churning through this new information. Finally Cherry said, "We should go. Why don't you and Peter join me aboard my ship for the trip to the Smokers galaxy."

"Sounds great," said Trixie, "have you named your ship yet?"

Cherry smiled, the pride evident on her round face though her oil-black eyes were unreadable as always. "As a matter of fact I call it Peter."

Her eyes drifted to Peter whose cheeks were as red as Cherry's skin color. She winked at him, making his neck also flush with color.

Trixie smiled to herself. She'd always thought there was something romantic between the two. "Great name," she said brightly. "Thanks for naming it after my son. I'm sure he's really honored. Aren't you son?" He nodded sheepishly, avoiding her gaze.

Trixie looked back to Cherry and they shared a smile. Cherry turned away and waved the palm of one hand over the side of the smooth, unblemished surface of the craft. A doorway large enough to allow a size XXL humanoid to enter glowed brightly then a section of the skin of the ship disappeared. Trixie couldn't see anything beyond the door but sensed the interior was larger than it looked on the outside. How this was possible, and the technology that made it possible, made her curious. She had to know more. Cherry hadn't just invented a new engine she appeared to have invented a new way to travel.

***

Upon entering the Peter (Trixie made a mental note to suggest the name of the ship be changed to the Bomb—entering anything named after her son was just too weird for words—she hoped Cherry would be okay with the change), Trixie's jaw dropped. Closing her eyes then opening then again, she had to blink to adjust to what she was seeing before her. A vast interior, set up to look exactly like the three-bedroom apartment she once owned in Dirt's capital city a very long time ago.

"Gee, Mom, have you ever seen a more beautiful vid theatre in your life?" said Peter, looking around in amazement after he stepped through the doorway to join her.

"And I see my favorite camping site near a mountain lake from my teen years," said Cherry.

Trixie gawked at Cherry in surprise. "What do you mean? It's a wonderful apartment I once owned on Dirt. I can hear the hum of the air car traffic through the open window overlooking the city skyline."

Trixie rushed across the sitting room, narrowly missing bumping into the ornately carved teak wood coffee table bordered by two leather wing chairs and a matching, full-sized sofa. On the floor beneath the furniture was a ruby red and dark green oriental carpet. Trixie could feel the soft carpet beneath her flats as she walked to the window. She closed her eyes when she stood in the open window, a soft, warm breeze splashing over her face. The smell of roses and daffodils permeated the air. "This place is amazing. Is this a holo-projection?" Trixie asked.

"No," said Cherry, "it's very real. At least real from each occupant's perspective. For each of us we see what we want to see. It's usually a favorite place or time from our subconscious. We can't influence the choice, it's done automatically based on the Peter's core memory scan when we boarded. The scan detected each of us, scanned us, and found memories of places that stimulated the pleasure center of each of our brains. The system then uploads the memory of that place and uses it to create the simulation you see before you. Each person sees something different, and it all occurs in a microsecond."

Trixie opened her eyes and turned to face Cherry. Behind her she heard the crunch of, and even detected the odor of, freshly buttered popcorn. Peter was enjoying his movie snack. How strange that this all seems so real. "It's fantastic, Cherry, but why the elaborate technology?"

It was then Trixie noticed the door had disappeared replaced by a wall with her favorite painting—two kittens playing tag with a flower. It was as if the doorway had never existed.

"I designed the interior for maximum comfort of the occupants during what I initially thought would be a very long trip. I assumed, based this on the time Lushites intergalactic vessels take to transit between galaxies, that it would take months, or if I had a major breakthrough, at least weeks to travel to other galaxies."

Trixie nodded, and after looking around selected a favorite wing chair facing the large window overlooking the sparkling Bellicose Tower. Cherry moved to sit in a matching chair to hers. Trixie shifted her weight, turning so she still faced her estranged friend. To Trixie's surprise, when Cherry sat down, the elegant, embroidered wing chair changed into an auburn red Adirondack chair. She isn't kidding. Wow. Amazing. "Makes sense."

Cherry eyes narrowed. "Yes, I thought so, too, until I had a more major than just major breakthrough." She paused, then added, "I discovered a way to create mini black holes and control them. Not only could I control their creation, size, and duration, but I could also control where they appeared in the universe. I discovered a way to use them to transport this ship to any location not only in this universe but also in others. A true doorway to multi-verses."

Trixie's heart beat faster and her mouth dried. Such technology in the wrong hands would make someone invincible. Whenever they wanted, they could transport to any place or time. The potential of such technology was both staggering and terrifying. Could we really have become that smart?

"We're here," Cherry said, standing. The chair instantly changed back into a wing chair as before.

"Where is here?" asked Trixie.

"Four. A planet near the rim of the Smokers galaxy. It's where your husband lives."

Chapter Fifteen

Winning is rad. The game is the only thing in life that counts for anything. Second place is for dbags. If you come second in this game you will kill yourself immediately.
– A pre-game instruction for Brainwashers XI - Suicide is Painless, circa 4413. (The game was banned in 4420, but is still played at rogue gamers' tournaments.)

"WE WANTED TO GO TO DIRT," said Trixie. "We wanted to see firsthand what happened while we've been away. And I had a few credits in a bank..." Her voice trailed off as she realized Cherry was staring at her. Her former head of security's pupiless eyes had always unnerved her.

"That no longer exists," finished Cherry. "Everything you knew in your former life is no more. The Smokers have polluted all that was good in your world and in this galaxy. The space itself is polluted with smoke and ash. The air on many of the habitable worlds is barely breathable, and the water is so toxic it has to be filtered ten times before it can be boiled for safe drinking water." Cherry shook her head and her eyes drooped to gaze at the floor.

"No, I'm afraid the curse of tobacco may have finally nailed the coffin lid shut on humankind for good."

Trixie rose from the chair and gazed out the window at the scene of air cars flitting amongst the sparkling towers dotting the skyline of the shining monument to all fast food had built. Cherry was right—the past was gone and all this was gone. There was nothing for her on Dirt, but they weren't on Dirt were they? Something wasn't right. "Why did you bring us to the planet where Herman lives? And how is Herman still alive? It's been more than a thousand years hasn't it?"

Cherry's mouth formed a wry smile. "It's ironic isn't it? Herman builds a ship that breaks the inter-dimensional barrier and by doing so extends your life, and he manages to develop a process that extends his own life using cryonics. Now, more than a thousand years after you parted company, you're together again."

"Mother, what is she talking about? I thought we'd see father again but he'd be a hologram or a clone. Is it really him? Uuuh, I mean the real him?"

Trixie looked at her son. "I'm as surprised as you are, Peter. But I guess we're about to be reunited with my husband, your father." Her eyes shifted to Cherry, who had two of her hands buried in the pockets of her lab coat. "I thought you were taking us to Dirt?" Trixie asked again.

Cherry shrugged. "I thought a slight detour to the planet Four might be a good idea first. After all you haven't been in this galaxy for a very long time, and I thought you might wish to see the person who sent you into another dimension before we met with Vice President Popover."

Trixie realized Cherry was right. She did want a few words with Herman.

While she wasn't angry with him anymore, she still wanted to tell him, and show him, how much she and Peter had changed since the last time they saw each other. "No worries, Cherry; actually I'm kind of looking forward to seeing him again."

From behind her she heard Peter suck in a breath. She scolded herself for spending the past few years bad-mouthing her ex-husband in front of her son. Until now she had never considered it rational that Peter would see his father again. She wiped the wince from her face and slowly turned to face the music and Peter. "Peter," she began, her heart beating rapidly in her chest, "I regret saying all those things about your father, but I thought he was dead. I had no idea he survived all this time." She averted her eyes. "Not in my wildest dreams we'd meet again. Sometimes the universe sends you a curve ball."

"A curve ball," Peter spat the words, an edge of bitterness evident in his voice. "My father and I had no relationship in the past, and we'll have none in the future. Ever." Peter's pale face became ruby red and his nostrils flared. "He sent us into another dimension! I've always suspected he hoped we'd be lost forever. I'm sure he's crapping himself now that we're here. He probably thinks we want revenge for what he did to us. And why not? Why don't we take revenge on his butt? Explain it to me, mother, and don't try to backtrack on all we talked about."

"Because there are far larger stakes than a family feud," interrupted Cherry.

"Like what, Dr. Bomb?" said Peter.

Cherry's dark eyebrows arched simultaneously on her forehead. "Like we've walked into the middle of a war."

Trixie and Peter stared wide-eyed at their former security chief with their mouths hanging open in surprise. War? Trixie swallowed hard. Oh, this is so not good.

***

They stood in Herman's house surveying the rustic accouterments while Mickey served tea in tiny, white, china cups. Trixie took her tea plain. She thanked the flying Purple as the fragrant odor of orange and pomegranate wafted over her senses, calming her nerves even before she had taken her first sip. Tea had always helped to calm her during stressful times. And a time of war was most definitely at the top of her stress meter.

"So, Herman, explain about this war," she said, shifting her gaze to lock eyes with her ex-husband who sat in an ornate wing chair near the massive stone fireplace. His gray-green eyes betrayed no emotion when they'd first been reunited after deboarding the Bomb. And he betrayed none of his feelings now as he explained the current situation.

The galaxy was the pawn of some powerful forces competing to rule it. Republic Vice President Jalapeño Popover craved power, and intended to crown himself emperor with the help of the military, who were conspiring with him to create a war between the Smokers and the Lushites. They planned to destroy the Lushites ship to spark the war, then declare martial law and seize power. After several months of cold war, Emperor Popover would petition the Lushites for peace and all would return to normal with the exception that Popover would retain control and declare himself emperor for life.

In the room with Trixie, listening to Herman's explanation, were her son, Peter, Piper Cleaner, the commandos commanding officer, Major Virginia Slim, also known as Major V, and her former security chief now brilliant propulsion scientist, Dr. Cherry Bomb. Nearby floated the holo-projection of one of the Brains, this one with an emerald green iris. The question was which of the Brains was this one?

Brains seemed to change eye color at a whim. Annoying, since it made identification impossible.

"Pardon me, but if I understand you correctly, Herman, this war hasn't actually started?" Trixie adjusted her bottom in the chair, realizing she hadn't moved since she sat down more than an hour ago.

"No, not yet, but an Admiral of the Grand Fleet is headed this way with an armada. His name is Reel Awesome and —"

"Ha, ha, you're playing us again." Peter moved to stand in front of his mother, his features twisted by anger. "You're going to believe this liar? He's a scumbag. Reel Awesome? That's not a reel name; he's made it up to trick us. There is no war coming. Maybe father intends to take over the galaxy himself." Peter snorted derisively. He turned to glare at Herman. "I don't believe a word of it. None."

Herman's eyes drooped at the corners and he emitted a heavy sigh. "Son. Peter, I don't blame you for not believing me. I did a bad thing to your mother and you. It was wrong, but believe me I'm trying to stop this war before it starts. I care about what happens to the galaxy, and I care about you."

Peter shook his head and his eyes welled with tears. "No way. I don't believe you."

"Maybe I can clear this up," interjected the Brain.

Trixie looked at the holo-projection. "How?"

"I'm the Admiral's Brain. I know everything he knows."

Peter stared at the AI, a frown creasing his brow. "OK," he said slowly, "Let's say we believe you; tell us what the admiral plans to do.

"Just as Herman told you the admiral is bringing a fleet to this system and he plans to wipe out not only the Lushite ship headed this way, but also to kill all of you including Herman and Mickey. Jal wants all potential opposition to his rule silenced and he's using the admiral to accomplish this end.

I know you think this planet is shielded and cloaked so you're safe here, unless..." The Brain said all this mater of factly, as if everyone knew these details, letting his words trail off meaningfully as he let them assume the cloaking system had been compromised, which it probably had.

Trixie scanned the faces of the other humanoids in the room. They'd been struck dumb by the Brain's revelation. "Well, now we know for sure what's coming. The larger question is what do we do about it?"

Major V scowled at her. "Well, we don't sit around and talk—we take action."

"Action?" asked Herman. "With what? We have a few commandos and no ships or guns. I don't build weapons; I build engines and experiment with cryonics and new food production methods and farming technology. War is not my thing."

"But we do have something that may help," interrupted Mickey, who floated nearby. "We have Bud Wiser."

Herman rolled his eyes and stood. He began to pace the room. "He's retired. He doesn't want anything to do with the galaxy anymore, not since they dumped him as emperor." Herman stopped and his brow wrinkled. He continued, "But if we could bring back the emperor, maybe he'd know what happened to the Warriors of the Slurp. Imagine if we had access to their mystic power for our side? Admiral Awesome wouldn't stand a chance against the power of the Slurp."

Peter looked at his mother. "A lot weird stuff must have happened since we've been gone," he said under his breath. Trixie offered her son a tight smile.

"What's this power of the Slurp?" she asked Herman.

Herman stopped pacing and faced his ex-wife. "It's kind of hard to explain. I've only read about it myself, but according to the legends, the Warriors of the Slurp move objects with their minds and can stop a man's heartbeat with the wave of one hand. Many people, including me, consider them magicians."

Trixie smirked. "Magic? Nonsense, there's no such thing. I'm surprised you'd believe such crap, you're a scientist."

Herman scowled. "Same old Trix. Always the skeptic. Well I'll prove I'm right. I'll bring Bud Wiser here. He'll tell you all about the Warriors' magic." Herman approached Cherry who sat silently on the gold-colored sofa across the room. Her dark eyes had been following Herman's pacing and now peered at him.

"Cherry, can you use that ship of yours to bring Bud here from Sector Two?" he asked.

Cherry looked thoughtful for a moment then nodded. "Yeah, I guess so, but someone's going to have to go through the wormhole to make Wiser enter it at the other end."

Major V smiled. "That would be my specialty."

Cherry chuckled. "OK, I'll need the planetary coordinates and we can get started immediately."

***

Major Virginia Slim suppressed a giggle as she stepped out of the wormhole—it tickled—into what appeared to be a Chinese food restaurant. There were Chinese waiters carrying large serving trays jammed with plates of steaming beef and broccoli, sweet and sour pork, steamed rice, and chow mien amid a myriad of round tables teaming with customers, all of them obese.

Stuck to the garish, fire-engine-red and gold walls, approximately a foot from the ceiling were plaster dragons painted gold.

Virginia blinked to clear her vision. The bright, tacky wallpaper hurt her eyes. *Where has Cherry sent me?*

As her vision cleared, she scanned the patrons and soon spotted her target, recognizing him from the digi-image the Brain had shown her. Bud was embroiled in a lively argument with the others diners at his table, greasy noodles trailing from his wide mouth. He laughed while trying to mumble around his food.

He had just speared and lifted two balls of sweet and sour boneless pork and was about to pop them into his mouth when his eyes drifted to Virginia and he stopped talking. His mouth hung open, his eyes wide. The fork in his cubby fingers slipped from his grip, landing on the plate with a sharp snap of metal on china. Suddenly he spat out the noodles.

We have a runner, thought Virginia. Her eyes narrowed and her hands formed fists. *I have a feeling I'm gonna love this. Kicking former royal butt made her day, every day.*

"Hold it right there, Wiser, don't move."

Bud pulled out the napkin he'd stuffed into the collar of his shirt as his beady eyes drifted to the swinging door to the kitchen then back to her. He started to rise to his feet when Major V rushed him. He'd managed to stand before she had her arms wrapped around his corpulent frame then she slammed him onto his back onto the carpeted floor with a dull thump.

Virginia's nose wrinkled. The odor of old grease coming from the carpet made her stomach twist with nausea. Climbing off the struggling fat man, she shoved him over onto his stomach and he flailed about trying to roll over. "Stop fighting me, Wiser, or I'll use your napkin to hog tie you and you won't be moving again."

"OK! OK!" Wiser screamed and he stopped fighting her. His breath came in gasps.

Breathing hard Virginia stood and studied her captive former emperor. Hard to believe he had ever been royalty. A fat man in a sweat-stained shirt who cried like a weak-kneed girl was hardly the type she would have thought of as an emperor. The restaurant was empty now, the customers having scattered like cockroaches under a noonday sun. The more likely scenario was the diners had been holographic projections and had simply disappeared when she shouted at Wiser.

Her well-honed sixth sense, sharpened by years of combat experience, told her this had been far too easy. Suddenly the door to the kitchen burst open and a Mark VIII armored security robot entered the restaurant's dimly-lit dining room. Its burnished steel body appeared gray against the garish wallpaper. It floated on an anti-grav field while it's ocular implants scanned the room. Virginia wondered who had signaled the bot, not that it mattered. The bot's duty was to rescue its boss, who was no doubt the sniveling worm of a humanoid at her feet.

Slowly extracting the pulse pistol from the holster on her hip, her eyes flitted to the charge indicator in the stock while her thumb flicked off the safety. Satisfied the weapon had plenty of charge, she gradually raised the barrel until she held it at eye level, aiming at where she knew the comm node was located atop the bot's cranial unit.

So far the robot hadn't made a threatening move in her direction. She slowly edged away from the prone former emperor, her eyes fixed on the hovering robot, intending to move to one of the tables she hoped to up end and use as a shield. Not that a cheap laminated table would do much to deflect the beam from the bot's energy weapon, but any small edge seemed worth trying at the moment. The Mark VIII models were legendary killers.

The robot's torso was round, about the size of a basketball. Sitting atop the torso was a pyramid-shaped head that swiveled three hundred and sixty degrees, giving it unlimited line of sight. The top of the pyramid housed a comm node with a high-speed processor for receiving and transmitting. The entire body was constructed from blast resistant materials, undoubtedly protected by an energy shield.

Major Slim's pistol would be like firing a peashooter at a brick wall. The robot was a highly effective and dangerous adversary for anyone threatening to attack its owner. Of course she wasn't interested in attacking Wiser just kidnapping him to take him to Pug's house on the other side of the planet.

It sounded so simple when I volunteered to do it, she mused.

After reaching the table farthest from the robot, she tipped it on its side spilling the plates filled with greasy Chinese food onto the carpet. One of the spring rolls tumbled to the floor and rolled across the carpet, coming to a stop within reach of Bud Wiser. Dishes, plates, and cutlery clattered, raining down from the table, scattering like chaff in the wind, fanning out across the carpet.

Gasping for air, Wiser had managed to stand. His face was a brilliant crimson and beads of shiny sweat dotted his pale forehead. He had the spring roll grasped in the sausage-like digits of his right hand. Popping the deep-fried pastry into his wide mouth, he chewed loudly with his mouth open so he could keep breathing while continuing to stuff himself. Major Slim winced at the sight, but she more had important problems right now than a fat man stuffing his face.

The robot moved across the room until it was between Wiser and her. Its ocular receptors were locked on her now. What was it waiting for? As if the bot could read her mind the front of its torso slid open and what she recognized as a Beta III disintegrator gun appeared and locked into place.

The distinctive hum coming from the gun signaled the bot had activated the weapon. It also meant she had only a few seconds before it fired and she was blown into atoms.

Her grip tightened around the butt of her pistol and she gritted her teeth, her jaw locked in determination. She wasn't about to go down without a fight.

"Hello," said Wiser who moved to an empty chair and sat down. "Who are you and what are you doing here?"

Virginia shifted her pistol to aim at the former emperor. "My name is Major Virginia Slim of the Order of the Gold Leaf Commandos. I'm here to bring you back with me to Herman Pug's house in Sector One."

Wiser's brow wrinkled. "Why?"

"We need your help to stop a war, and none of us thought you'd agree to come along voluntarily." Virginia shrugged then continued, "So we decided kidnapping was the only way to bring you back. We're short on time and options."

Surprisingly, Wiser smiled, wiping his greasy hand on his stained trousers. "All you had to do was ask. Back in the old days saving the galaxy was my specialty."

***

Stepping out of the wormhole, Virginia, grasping Wiser by his sweaty arm, was greeted to the genteel scene of Herman, Peter, Trixie, and Cherry seated in wing chairs sipping tea by the glowing fire in the stone fireplace. The Purple sat on the back of the sofa. It looked asleep, not that anyone would be able to tell if the alien slug was sleeping or dead. The holo-image of the Brain was nowhere to be seen. Piper Cleaner was also absent.

As if on cue, the Purple suddenly extended its wings and floated off its temporary perch. "Welcome back, Major, I see your mission was successful."

Herman was first out of his chair to greet the new arrival. "Welcome, Emperor Wiser, I'm Herman Pug. This is my house."

Wiser wheezed coughed then said, "I know who you are. And thank you for the welcome. Do you have any food by chance?"

Herman smiled. "I don't normally have the kind of food you would like, but I can have the Brain create some for you."

Wiser's eyes went wide and his puffy face flushed red. "You have a Brain?"

Peter rushed to Wiser's side and guided the obviously distressed former royal to the sofa. Once he was seated, he seemed to gather himself and his features gradually drained of color as his breathing steadied.

Herman walked to stand over Wiser. "I'm sorry if I upset you. I thought everyone had a Brain."

Wiser shook his head, his jowls swaying in time to his movements. "Not me. I hate the things. They caused me no end of grief when I ruled the galaxy. I once tried to shut them down by sabotaging that planet of theirs, but they banded together and...." His voice trailed off and his beady eyes surveyed the room. "It's not here is it?"

Herman offered a tight-lipped smile and sat next to him on the sofa. "No. He's busy elsewhere. Go on, please."

Wiser's cheeks puffed out as he released the air from his lungs. "OK, but if the Brains get wind of what I'm about to tell you, they're not going to be very happy with me." He avoided Herman's eyes. "And I'm going to be in a little trouble with you all, too."

Trixie, who until now had remained silent listening to Wiser's story rose from the chair and now stood one hand resting against the mantel of the fireplace, finally spoke up. "Why would you be in trouble with us?'

The former emperor sighed. "I lied. There never were Warriors of the Slurp. The Brains helped me create the myth. When I turned on them, they started the story that the WOS had disappeared. I had no choice but to flee into exile or the Brains would have disappeared me for real."

Virginia stared at the emperor her brow creased by a scowl. "You perpetrated a fraud on the entire galaxy?" Wiser nodded. "You are really a piece of work, Wiser."

Trixie moved to stand beside the major and placed a hand on her shoulder. Glancing up at her, the major saw the look in Trixie's eyes and realized they were not only allies, but decided she better back off, for now. Her eyes shifted to lock on Wiser's "OK, but when this is over you and I are going to have a serious talk."

"I was CEO of Heavenly Sky Burger back in the day," Trixie said, "so I know about taking charge. The problem we have now is the Brains are working together toward some mysterious goal we haven't yet been able to discover."

Peter interrupted his mother, "But don't they plan to take over the galaxy?"

Trixie nodded. "For sure that's true but why? They're AI's, they have no need for food, sex, money, or any other things that have caused humanoid wars for millennia. And their home planet is about as secure as it can be made. They are confident no one can access their central processors."

Trixie's eyes narrowed and Virginia's heart froze. Trixie was correct.

It had to mean the Brains were working for someone else but who?

"So who's behind this?" asked Virginia. "Reel Awesome?"

Trixie scowled. "No, I don't think so, but you know him better than I do. What do you think?"

Virginia shook her head. "No, I don't think he's smart enough or connected enough to pull this off by himself. He's always followed orders, I doubt the Brains would entrust him with their future. He's just too easily swayed by money, power, or anything that distracts him from the goal right in front of him. He has no imagination."

"Say, where's Piper?" asked Peter.

"I thought he was in the bathroom," said Cherry.

"He's been gone a long time," said Herman his brow wrinkling. "Mickey where's Piper?"

The Purple flapped his wings gently until he was in the middle of the room where he floated for several seconds before he said, "He's left the planet in the Flash-O-Matic 5000 we have been keeping secret and is currently in orbit. He intends to crash the ship into Admiral Awesome's command ship."

"I guess that ship not such a big secret after all," said Cherry sardonically.

The purple floated to the center of the room. "Humans. Always causing trouble."

Chapter Sixteen

"This report confirms tobacco is a plant. Plants are good. Good is good. Therefore using this perfect logic as our guide, smoking tobacco is good."

– Excerpt from a speech by the President of Galaxy Tobacco after the Galactic Surgeon Admiral released a report concerning the health risks of smoking, circa 3939.

THE PILOT OFFICER SEATED at his station on the bridge of the Grand Fleet's flagship noticed the blip on his screen where the sensors only seconds before registered empty space. Somehow the incoming vessel had appeared from nowhere. He'd wondered if the so-called phantom planet actually existed. This may have proved it did. Plotting the course of the ship now heading toward them in ever-increasing speed back to its projected point of origin, he marked the spot where the planet might be located.

Swiveling his chair to face the Admiral's command chair behind him, he made his report. "Sir, we have an incoming vessel. Its speed is increasing. Current projections indicate it will intercept us in twenty-three minutes.

I traced the craft to its point of origin and marked the coordinates." He turned back to his board and locked his eyes on the projected path of the incoming craft. "The AI projects it is on a collision course."

Admiral Awesome cleared his throat. "Will our shielding protect us?"

At her station to the pilot's left the weapons officer shook her head. "Not at the speed the AI estimates it will be travelling when it intersects with us. Also, by the time we power up the pulse generators and create a firing solution it will be too late."

"You mean with all the technology and experience at our fingertips, a single vessel will destroy this ship, killing all of us?" the Admiral said the indignation evident in his tone.

"Yes sir," replied the pilot officer, his voice calm and even.

"Well, I'm not one to give up so easily. Comm officer," the admiral said to the communications officer, Cuke Roller, an alien recruited for the fleet from the Sushi world, Kelp III, "send out a signal to anyone nearby and request assistance. Then send a message on a tight beam directly at the incoming vessel."

"Yes, sir," replied Roller, "but what do you wish me to say to the pilot of the enemy ship?"

The pilot officer swiveled his chair to face the admiral again. Awesome had a wry grin on his features, which struck him as odd. "Tell the pilot we are carrying a recently manufactured synthetic mineral aboard our ship, which when detonated will destroy not only both of us but this entire system of planets. Their star will go nova."

The pilot's eyes narrowed. "But, sir, that's not true. There is no such mineral."

Awesome eyed him. "You and I know that, pilot officer, but the person aboard that ship doesn't know if this true or not. Uncertainty may save us yet."

Looking away Awesome said, "Send the messages immediately."

Roller and the pilot officer shared a look of doubt, then the comm officer shrugged and sent both messages as ordered.

The pilot officer transferred the view of projected path of the enemy ship onto the main vid screen making up the wall at the front of the bridge. He also added a digital countdown clock at the top right corner. It now read twenty minutes, seven seconds. The path of the enemy vessel was depicted as a red line against the black star field. With each passing second it grew ever closer. The message they'd just sent seemed to have made no difference to its course.

Oh well, he thought, it was worth a try I guess.

Suddenly two large blips appeared at the edge of the star field. They were obviously large and fast, since they quickly shot across the screen and now bracketed the incoming vessel. Tapping his sensor controls he peered at the readouts on the small screen recessed into his station in front of him. What he saw made his heart skip a beat as he swallowed hard. It couldn't be. He rechecked the readings, and when the results came back the same he realized they were in deeper trouble than a single ship on a collision course.

"Sir! Two more ships have appeared. They've bracketing the first ship. They're Lushites, sir." The pilot officer looked over his right shoulder at the Admiral. His commander appeared uncertain, his hands trembled. The admiral wasn't going to be much help.

Looking back to the large vid screen he watched in rampant fascination as the two Lushite ships guided the smaller vessel to a new course, away from them. They must have used some sort of tractor beam or force field to encapsulate the smaller ship. A knot formed in the pilot officer's stomach. The power necessary to accomplish this had to be off the charts. The amount of energy output according to the readings was greater than the output of their entire fleet.

They were more outclassed than he'd thought when this mission was first proposed.

During the mission briefing, the intelligence officer talked about the potential capabilities of a Lushite vessel. Since they hadn't seen a Lushite ship in more than a thousand years a lot could have changed, so the intelligence officer had been vague about the effectiveness of the Lushites weapons and defensive measures.

What he saw now made him think they were the flies and the Lushite vessels were the flyswatters. Clearly surrender was the only option if they were going to survive this encounter.

"Pilot officer," began the admiral his voice trembling slightly, "plot us an intercept course to the point of origin of those ships. After setting course, increase speed to maximum. We'll ram whatever is hidden behind that energy screen. The mystery planet is real after all. Its our duty to destroy that world and save the galaxy from chaos." The admiral paused and Roller could hear him releasing a ragged breath. "Order the rest of the fleet to follow us. We will end this war before it starts."

"Sir, may I speak freely?" asked Roller. The admiral nodded his approval, his dark eyes hard as lumps of coal. "To what end are we taking this action, sir?"

The admiral's jaw tightened. "The combined energy of the fleet's ships' reactors will explode when we crash into the hidden planet, thus wiping out the enemy before they attack Dirt." His commanding officers eyes narrowed. "Our job is to destroy them with every resource at our disposal and that's exactly what I intend to do."

"Aye, aye, sir," replied Roller her tone edged with the pride born of being a fleet officer about to die in the line of duty. The pilot officer stiffened. She and the admiral were correct.

We must all do our duty even when we face certain death.

After adjusting their course, and accepting a nod from the comm officer that the fleet had acknowledged the new orders, he pressed his hand flat on the console sending the engines of the warship instructions to come to full thrust.

The deck plates underfoot shivered and the mighty warship leapt forward increasing speed exponentially with each passing second. They would never be able to achieve the speed of the three enemy ships, but the pilot officer hoped their sudden course change and increase in speed had surprised the enemy enough they would be able to complete their mission. It was clear if they failed, then the mission failed. Simple.

Any way you sliced this they were going to die; the only question would be would their deaths be with honor or with futility? I might as well flip a coin, Roller thought as he turned to face his console again.

***

"Brain!" Virginia barked.

Herman's Brain popped into existence, his holo-image this time a human sized pink bunny with long, white-tipped ears. The holo bunny sat on its haunches, its brown eyes peering at them. It some ways it was better than the eyeball holo but Virginia would have preferred a humanoid shape.

"You rang?" said the Brain a deep throaty voice coming from the bunny.

Virginia shook off the feeling of stupid the AI deserved right now. "Are there any vessels at the Lushite way station?" She looked at Trixie and offered her a tight smile. "I listen when people talk." Trixie grinned.

"Yes," replied the Brain. "There are two Lushite intergalactic vessels currently at the way station in Sector Three."

"How long have they been there?"

"For five years, six months, two weeks, and six point three hours."

Virginia nodded. "Contact the captain's of those ships and display both of them on the main vid screen in Herman's lab. Tell them it's urgent I speak with them about a matter of life and death. We'll be there in two minutes."

"Of course," replied the Brain before the holo-bunny shimmered and disappeared.

Virginia scanned the group. Trixie and Peter looked eager to help, as did Herman. Cherry's hands had formed four fists. Bud's complexion had paled to the color of fresh snow.

"Bud, you stay here and think of a way to use the myth you and the Brains created. When we return you better have some idea how we're going to stop Jal from taking over the galaxy. The rest of you come with me, we'll stop Awesome."

As they started for the lift to Herman's underground laboratory, Virginia gripped Trixie's arm and held her a few paces behind the rest of the group. Speaking in low tones she said, "Trixie, I'm going to need your help talking to those Lushite captains. I suspect addiction has bad memories for you, but you understand better than anyone how to deal with the irrational."

"What do you intend to tell them?"

"I was thinking of telling them Piper stole our supply of bar snacks and asking them help us get them back." Trixie nodded her eyes uncertain.

"What? Should I try something else?"

Trixie shrugged. "I think they'll need more incentive than ancillary items to their addiction. In my opinion you should tell them the truth about what's been happening and that their liquor supply will be cut off under a new Emperor's rule."

Virginia cocked an eyebrow. "So the truth followed by a lie?"

Trixie smiled. "We don't know if Jal will cut off any visiting Lushites' liquor supply, but it's a fair guess. He is a tobacco addict, after all. And how do the Lushites know for sure?"

"What about the Brains? Won't they interfere and tell the Lushites' Brains what we're up to?" asked Virginia.

"Brain," said Trixie. The pink bunny appeared once again. "Did you tell the Lushites Brains about us?"

"No," replied the bunny. The holo-image shimmered slightly then the virtual image steadied. "Actually we tried, but they are the most disagreeable Brains we have ever encountered. They weren't interested in the least in joining us to take over the galaxy. Do you believe it they actually enjoy serving the Lushites?"

Virginia chuckled. "So we call what we tell the Lushites speculation based on facts not readily apparent? I like it, it works for me."

The lift soon let them out in Herman's vast laboratory complex, far below the planet's surface. They stood before the wall sized vid screen, looking at the images of the two Lushite captains. One, who said her name was Peppermint Schnapps, had long blonde hair cascading over her petite shoulders, and was dressed in a puffy white shirt and tight black pants, with a sword in a sheath hanging from her hip. Her emerald green eyes were watchful and her thin lips had formed a sneer.

The other captain was a bulbous man, his baldhead shiny with a sheen of perspiration. He held a large glass mug in one hand, from which he took frequent sips as Virginia explained the situation with Jal.

"We're running out of time," murmured Mickey, who floated just out of view of the screen. Trixie suggested there was no point in alerting the Lushites to the presence of a telepathic Purple. The Lushites might be alcoholics but they weren't stupid.

Trixie shot a warning look at her ex-husband who shushed the alien slug.

Finally Virginia came to the point of their call. "We need your help. We don't have a ship capable of intercepting the small ship, which I'm certain your readouts show is headed for the incoming fleet. We would appreciate if you would intercept that ship and bring it back here."

"What has any of this to do with us?" said the female captain, her tone condescending. This was going to be tougher than she first thought.

"The smaller ship will provide the means to defeat anyone who opposes Jal. As part of Jal's plan, it is important they destroy your ships. When Jal takes over as Emperor he will ban alcohol from the galaxy. You Lushites will not be allowed in this galaxy ever again."

The fat man stopped in mid sip and started to cough as if he were choking. When he managed to speak again, he said, "But we need this way station. Bud Wiser negotiated this stop with us over a millennia ago. It's an important resupply port on the way to the Rum Nebula. We party there."

As she had suspected, these Lushites hadn't been to their galaxy in a very long time. "Couldn't you just go another way?" suggested Virginia. While she could have played up this concern, it had to be for logical reasons the Lushites took action.

Captain Schnapps smirked. "We've been going this way for over a thousand years; why would we change now?"

Virginia shared a decisive look with Trixie. They had the hook set and now was the time for the landing of the fish. Or should I say the boozer, thought Virginia.

"OK then, please take your ships to the coordinates we sent to your nav system..." she caught Herman's nod from the corner of one eye, "...we need that ship stopped and brought back."

"No worries," said the fat captain, unsuccessfully trying to suppress a muffled burp. His half of the screen went dark. Looking none too happy, Captain Schnapps offered a terse nod then her half of the screen also went dark.

Virginia locked eyes with Herman. "Can you show the course of the ships on the big screen?" Herman nodded and waved one hand at Mickey who floated over to hover above a console near where they stood. Immediately the large wall-sized screen came to life, displaying a representation of Four's system of five planets and six moons.

Green triangles represented the grand fleet headed by Admiral Awesome; the Flash-O-Matic 5000 was represented by a glowing red square, while the two Lushite ships were flashing yellow circles. The yellow circles quickly overtook the red square and managed to steer it away from its intended target, the cluster of green triangles.

Virginia closed her eyes and released a sigh of relief. Disaster had been avert... "Hold on," Mickey said sharply.

The major opened her eyes and was horrified to see the green mass had changed course and increased speed. They were now on a suicide run to wipe out Four and them with it.

"Herman, will the shielding surrounding the planet hold if they crash into it with all those ships?"

"Truthfully I don't know. The shield wasn't designed to repel a force that size. Frankly, I never thought I was important enough to warrant such attention. Mickey tells me what the admiral's thinking. Is he serious, or is this a game?"

"No, it's not a game. He's going to kill us all. He thinks this is his duty, if you can believe it."

Virginia swallowed hard and her heart beat hard in her chest. She had to think. "How much time until impact?" she asked.

"According to these readings, twelve minutes," said Herman.

Virginia's mind whirled with possibilities. There had to be some way to stop them. "What about the two Lushite vessels? Do they have time to intercept?"

"Yes, but they won't be able to stop the entire fleet, and it will be tight even if they try."

Suddenly a third yellow flashing circle appeared, directly in the path of the onrushing fleet. Another Lushite vessel? thought Virginia.

"I'm picking up a transmission, "said Herman, his voice edged with excitement. "It's someone named Smokey Cigarillo. She's ordered Admiral Awesome to stand down."

"Look they're slowing!" shouted Peter.

Sure enough the green mass of ships was slowing and changing course away from the energy shield guarding Four. Virginia's shoulders relaxed and her heart rate decreased. "Contact that ship find out who this Smokey person is. I want to talk to her as soon as possible."

Peter slapped his father on the back and Herman gazed at his son, the love evident in his eyes. Trixie ran to embrace her ex-husband and her son, wrapping both in her arms. The three Pugs laughed and cried simultaneously. They hugged and laughed with obvious joy.

The Purple floated toward her, stopping to hover near Virginia's right shoulder. Eyeing the Purple, Virginia whispered, "What do you think?"

"I don't have to think," replied the alien, "I read minds ya know. It looks like what was once broken has been joined together once again."

Virginia looked at the Purple in surprise. "A romantic? Who would have thought?"

"What can I say?" said Mickey with a giggle. "I had a lot of time to read while Herman slept.

"Who is Smokey Cigarillo?" asked Cherry.

"She's the liaison with the Lushite vessel that started this mess when it entered the galaxy," said Virginia. "Why?"

"They aren't Lushites," interjected Mickey. "They're Gamers. They play Virtual Reality games in pods. They only came to this galaxy to discover the status of the first Lushite ship from a thousand years ago—the one Bud Wiser the First arrived on. The ship is a rental."

Virginia sat in one of the empty chairs in front of the command console that controlled the vid screen. "So why is Cigarillo still aboard that ship? And why isn't it on it's way to Dirt?" Nothing in these events made sense. A thought occurred to Virginia. "The Lushites no longer controlled their galaxy, do they?"

Trixie released her newly reunited family from her embrace and moved to stand in front of the large wall vid screen. The joy on her angular features had been replaced with a look of concern. "Yes, that's true. The Gamer Alliance controls their galaxy now. The Lushites make a nice living renting their ships for gamers' cruises', virtual weddings, conventions, and tournaments. Is this important?"

"Yes, I think so. I suspect Smokey is an agent for Jal. I don't know what exactly she's up to, but she may have already made an agreement with the gamers that will further the new emperor's ends."

"You are really good," said a husky feminine voice behind them. Turning as one the group found themselves facing the woman Virginia knew as Smokey Cigarillo. In her hands she held a pulse rifle, and flanking her were very tall, very armored soldiers hefting heavy blast weapons. The guns were leveled at them. The expression worn by the burly soldiers suggested they better not move too fast or they'd be dust. Nothing needed to be said; message received loud and clear.

Virginia moved her hand to rest it on the butt of her holstered pistol and grinned at the new arrival. "Smokey, how nice to see you again. And thanks for the compliment. High praise coming you from you."

Smokey smirked and her green eyes sparkled. She moved to cradle her gun in one arm and had a thin cigar between her lips and lit using only one hand within seconds. "Major, you violated your orders." She shook her head, never letting her eyes drift away from the commando. "Where's the rest of your team?" Virginia shook her head. She wasn't about to give this woman any information. Smokey shrugged. "Not that it matters. I won't be here long enough for your tiny force to stop me."

She looked at Cherry. "Is this your wormhole ship?" she said titling her head slightly at the cube-shaped ship in the middle of the laboratory.

Cherry gritted her teeth. "I hope you're not planning to steal it. That would be highly dangerous. I'm the only one who can pilot the ship safely."

Smokey smiled and cocked one eyebrow. A stream of smoke came from between her full lips. "That's exactly what I had in mind, actually. You'll take us to Dirt." The smile and all signs of congeniality disappeared from her features.

Dropping her cigar she stepped on it then hefted her gun in both hands again and pointed it at Cherry. "Let's go." She waved the gun barrel encouraging Cherry to move toward the vessel. "Now."

Virginia considered pulling her gun, but the two soldiers would cut her down before her pistol cleared the holster. No, she decided to wait. She would see Smokey again. Next time she was determined to have the advantage.

Cherry, prodded by Smokey's rifle, disappeared into the cube-shaped craft and the two soldiers backed up the ramp until they, too, disappeared. It didn't take long for the ship to pop from existence as if it had never been.

***

Jal drew the smoke into his lungs as his eyes darted to the blank screen sitting on his desk. He shifted his weight in his executive chair. It had been too long. His well-tuned mind, ideally made for scheming, was sending him warning signals. Something had gone wrong.

Stubbing out his cigarette in the crystal ashtray on his desk he then shifted forward in the chair. He pressed an index finger on his screen and it came to life. The usual image of his favorite cigar appeared. He swiped the bit of drool that came out the side of his mouth with his tongue then said, "Brain, activate the long range comm."

His request was met with silence.

His heart rate increased and beads of sweat sprung out on his forehead. Now he was scared. He shivered. He had only had this feeling once before in his life. The day of the great tobacco fire on Weed Wacker III, when half of the supply of tobacco plants in the Algorithm system was wiped out. A terrible day indeed, but somehow this felt worse.

"Brain!" Still no answer. Jal gritted his teeth. Damn that pile of memory chips and diodes. When I get my hands on his programming I'm gonna...

The floor trembled and the windows of his office overlooking the city seemed to undulate like ocean waves. Jal jumped up and rushed to look over the towers of glass and plasti-steel that spread out to the horizon. Peering at the sky, he realized it looked strange. It had the reddish hue of sunset yet it was only eleven in the morning. Was the sky on fire?

Though his office was air-conditioned, the air was suddenly warm—and getting warmer with each passing second.

Racing to his desk, he plunked down in his chair and activated his screen manually. The manual digital interface keyboard appeared on the surface of his desk. He quickly keyed in the emergency code.

A man dressed like a pirate appeared on his screen. His bloodshot eyes had trouble focusing and he wobbled; yet he was apparently seated. "Yeah," he said, his speech slurred by what Jal knew was alcohol.

"Captain, I need your help," Jal said.

"Name's Cap'n Jack...whas you want?"

"I need a lift. You're the only one that can help me."

Captain Jack Daniels the Fifth held one finger to his lips. "No need to shout, bucko, I'll get me first officer. Hold on." The captain stood on shaky legs, then stumbled to the left side of the screen, disappearing from view.

A woman appeared, dressed in a loose-fitting pink blouse. She had a head full of pink curls the color of cotton candy and her eyes were ruby red. "Hi, she said brightly obviously not as inebriated as her captain, though her cheeks were slightly flushed. "This is Aloha Screwdriver, first mate of the L.S.S. Shot. What can I do for ya?"

"I need to get off planet now," said Jal.

One of Aloha's pink eyebrows rose slightly. "OK, I can see that. Our sensors show your sun has gone nova. You probably have twenty-five minutes until your atmosphere boils away. But why should we give you a lift?"

"My name's Jalapeño Popover. My ancestor helped you guys, and I thought now you could help me."

Aloha looked thoughtful for a few seconds then she smiled. "Makes sense. Brain, transport him aboard."

As the familiar tingle of the Lushite MASS transport beam gripped him, Jal made himself a promise. He would find whoever was behind this treachery and make them pay dearly, or he wasn't Jalapeño Popover, the next emperor of the galaxy.

***

"What do we do now?" asked Trixie.

Virginia's eyes narrowed and her fingers tightened around the butt of her pistol. She had no idea. The briefing team had never provided this scenario. Someone had gone off script.

The only good news from these events was the war had been averted. She glanced at the large vid screen and saw the green triangles representing the grand fleet, the third Lushite ship accompanying them, were headed out of the system. Her eyes flitted to the Pugs. The other good news was that a family had been reunited and renewed. The odd thing was how the war and Jal's rise as emperor had been relatively easily averted. It made her suspicious.

"Brain," she said.

The pink holo-bunny appeared. "Yes, major?"

"We will need transportation to Dirt. Can you arrange it?"

"Yes, immediately." The bunny disappeared again.

Virginia nodded and she studied the two flashing yellow circles bracketing the Flash-O-Matic 5000 headed back to Four. They all seemed to be taking their sweet time.

Suddenly the three markers erupted in a flash of light and they were gone. They'd been destroyed. The crews of the Lushite ships and her friend Piper Cleaner were dead.

"Brain!" she snapped. The AI bunny reappeared. Virginia glared at the Brain's holo-image. "Something's happened. What?" The AI didn't respond immediately. "Now!" she ordered.

"Uhhh...I'm sorry, major, but a terrible thing has occurred. Too terrible to image."

Virginia's stomach muscles tightened. "Tell me." Sweeping one arm to indicate the others standing nearby. "Tell us all."

"Dirt's sun has gone nova. The planetary system has been destroyed, absorbed by the star's expansion. All life in the system has been wiped out. Over sixty billion lives gone."

Virginia ground her teeth. "Jal," she growled.

"No," said the AI. "It was Smokey. A black hole injected a device into the star's core which caused a chain reaction resulting in the supernova"

"And you know this how?" asked Herman.

"Those two soldiers with Smokey were holo-projections used by two of my colleague Brains. They sent me a signal when their mission to take out Dirt and Vice President Popover was complete."

Trixie's eyes widened. "You Brains are helping Smokey to double-cross...everyone."

"Yes."

Virginia sighed. It made perfect sense. Smokey had learned well from the VR gamer addicts how to create realistic illusions. She should have suspected this from the beginning.

Pulling a cigarette from the field pouch on her hip, Virginia lit the tip with the lighter from another pouch. She eased back in the form fitted ergo chair and took a long drag of the fragrant tobacco.

Closing her eyes she wondered what the galaxy would be like with its first female emperor. It couldn't be any worse than a male emperor could it?

Epilogue

"It's all about me."

— Statement to the media by Perky Perfection, part-time leader of the Shallows League of the Self-Absorbed. (Her statement is brief since she was late for an urgent appointment with her Self Image Coach.)

December 4444 1/4

Former Major Virginia Slim removed a helmet that barely contained her flowing curls of blonde hair as she sat in the chair across from Trixie Pug in the living room of Herman's house on Four. After Smokey declared herself Empress for life, Four had been invaded by ten squads of the Order of the Gold Leaf Commandos who supervised the stripping of every piece of technology Herman had created. The planet's defensive screens and invisibility field had been compromised, and Herman and the Purple had been taken back to Smokey's palace on Dirt II. No one knew what happened to Piper Cleaner, but everyone presumed he was dead.

The commandos had been unable to capture Dr. Cherry Bomb, but they desperately wanted to find her. Virginia had protected the brilliant scientist, and helped to hide her from the Brains and Empress Smokey's commandos. She was determined the empress and her henchmen would never get their hands on Cherry.

"So what's the news?" asked Trixie before she lifted her teacup and took a sip of the fragrant jasmine brew.

Virginia offered a tight, grim smile. "Their soldiers aren't close to finding Cherry, but I'm concerned they may yet make Mickey tell them where she's hiding."

Trixie nodded, her lips forming a thin line and her brow creased. "I share your concern, but Herman assures me the Purple can be creative when someone he doesn't like tries to force him. His Achilles heel is his loyalty to Herman, but they can't very well threaten him as long as he keeps providing them with the technical expertise they need."

Virginia shifted her weight in her chair. "Are the rumors true?"

Surprising her Trixie chuckled. "So I'm told. They've inadvertently opened wormholes to other galaxies and the results are, shall we say, varied."

"How many species have they catalogued so far?" asked Virginia.

"About fifty reported by our network of spies. So far the only ones we know of for sure are The Shallows League of the Self-Absorbed, The Couch Potatoes Confederacy, The Vegan Union, and The Meat Lovers Federation, but they appear to be causing diplomatic chaos for the new empress."

Virginia chuckled. "Good, that will keep her off-balance while we gather our forces for the rebellion."

"You do realize, Virginia, the empress holds all the cards right now. She's manipulating the supply of each group's addiction and using the access to control key personnel throughout the galaxy. It's going to be a long haul."

Virginia nodded. Without warning, her forehead was suddenly covered in beads of perspiration and her hands trembled. Her head pounded and her heart rate increased as her stomach did somersaults. She wondered if the craving for cigarettes would ever leave her. "I could really use that cup of tea you offered earlier," she whispered.

Trixie stood and went to the teacart near the stone fireplace. She poured a fresh cup for her friend, then delivered it to the side table next to Virginia's wing chair. After cupping the cup in both hands, Virginia lifted the warm china to her lips and took a sip. The fragrant tea invaded her senses and the wave of nausea and sweats immediately subsided.

Opening her eyes, she looked into her friend's, who now stood over her with a look of concern on her features. She smiled weakly. "Withdrawal is hell." She swallowed hard then added, "Even if it takes a thousand years, we have to take back the galaxy from this tyrant."

Even as the words slipped from between her lips Virginia doubted she'd ever see a free galaxy again in her lifetime. All she had to motivate her was hope. Her eyes flitted to Trixie. Hope and good friends.

The Lushites will return...

About the Author

International selling author, Russ Crossley writes romance under the name R.G. Hart, mystery/suspense under the name R.G. Crossley, and science fiction and fantasy under his own. This year there will be re-issues the romantic comedies, Bachelorette: Zombie Edition and Antique Virgin by 53rd Street Publishing, paranormal romantic comedy, Zomopolis, and a new western romance entitled, The Fire In Their Hearts co-authored with R.S. Meger will be published in 2013 by Champagne Books. Also, look for another Aloha adventure, Bloody Betty Queen of the Pirates, coming later in 2013.

In addition the near future suspense novel, The Last Serial Killer by R.G. Crossley was recently released by 53rd Street Publishing in ebook and trade paperback versions early in 2013.

His latest science fiction satire set in the far future, Revenge of the Lushites, is a sequel to Attack of the Lushites released in 2011. The latest title in the series will be released in the fall of 2013. Both titles are available in e-book and trade paperback.

He has sold several short stories that have appeared in anthologies from Pocket Books, St. Martins Press, at Smashwords, Amazon, and other e-retail sites.

With his wife, romance author R.S. Meger, he owns and operates a small press publishing company, 53rd Street Publishing. The company began in April 2011 and now has over one hundred e-book titles and over twenty-five print titles, with more planned in 2013 and 2014.

He is a member of SF Canada and the Greater Vancouver Chapter of Romance Writers of America.

He is also an alumni of the Oregon Coast Professional Fiction Writers Master Class taught by award winning author/editors, Kristine Katherine Rusch and Dean Wesley Smith.

To find a complete listing of his work check out his website http://www.rghart.com, http://russstory.blogspot.com.Razor's blog can be found at http://razorandedge.blogspot.com

Feel free to contact him on Facebook or Twitter. He loves to hear from readers

Other books by the Author

Titles as R.G. Crossley

Short Stories

Razor and Edge Mysteries
The Kidnapping of Billy Buttons
String of Pearls
Death by Clown
Beggin' For Murder
Ragged Ice
The Grand Central Mystery
A Strange Case of Undead Murder

Jazz Stiletto Mysteries
A Day Without Sunshine
Skullduggery

Non-Series Mysteries
Mirror Image
Dangerous Waters
Cape Disappointment
Boomerang
The Watcher of Wayburn Street
The Apprentice
Drip!
A Beautiful Friendship and The Parrot of Doom
Robine's Diary
The Christmas Club
Loose Ends
Splatter Pattern
It Takes Two

"I loved this book. Mr. Crossley has a wonderful way of combining both off-the-wall humor and exciting adventure. I enjoyed all the characters. I thought they were well developed, and even the worst if them had a little bit of saving grace hidden inside. I found myself becoming attached to them and wanting to learn more about them.

The Lushites were my favorites. When I read the description of their leader Jack, I couldn't help but think of Captain Jack Sparrow. Laughing, I could just picture him swaying across the deck.

My favorite character had to be Bud. His interaction with both The Brain and Jal were wonderful. I loved the fact that with all the individuals who held the power and ran the different worlds, it was Bud and Jal who ended up the heroes.

"Underneath all the humor and action ran a thread of warning. A thread
about excess and the consequences of that excess, whether it be overeating, drinking or smoking. All in all a very witty, over-the-top story with a moral warning.

Mr. Crossley's writing reminds me a great deal of the writings of Lionel Fenn, aka Charlie Grant, and like Mr. Fenn, left me smiling and wanting more." — ladybug, Amazon.com

Praise for RG Hart's "My Partner the Zombie" in the zombie romance anthology, Hungry For Your Love from St Martin's Press

"Filled with stories from the hilarious to the horrific ... there is something here to tug at the hearts (and brains) of any zombie lover. Highly recommended for anyone's collection." — Monsterlibrarian. com"

"Unrequited love is hard to accept, but Aloha Armstrong knows that she has only herself to blame.

"Being a Zombie is not an easy existence, but Matt Butcher is resigned to making it the best it can be.

Following up on a story of attempted murder puts Matt and Aloha in the path of a madman. They must ferret out the truth before more people are infected with the virus. Aloha wants the man caught, but she is devastated that she could very well lose Matt in the process. There is a great dynamic between Matt and Aloha, and it really makes for some fun reading." http://coffeetimeromance.com/BookReviews/hungryforyourlove.html — Coffee Time Romance — (4 cups)"

"A wonderfully twisted undertaking (pun intended), 'Hungry for Your Love' is a many-faceted feast of love, loss, sex, heartbreak, rotting flesh, and romance from beyond the grave." — Christopher Golden, bestselling author and editor of The New Dead"

Praise for Russ Crossley's Attack of the Lushites

"The first time I read Attack of the Lushites, I was shaking my head by page two and laughing out loud by page five. One of the wildest, craziest, and most entertaining novels I have had the pleasure to read." — Dean Wesley Smith, USA Today bestselling author

Anthologies
The Adventures of Razor and Edge:
Five Tales From The Quirky Detective Team

Novels
A Bad Case of Loyalty
The Last Serial Killer
Shear Murder

Titles as Russ Crossley

Novels
Attack of the Lushites
Revenge of the Lushites

Short Stories
Countdown
Shoeless Moe
Round Up At The Burger Bar:
The Story of Trixie Pug, Parts 1, 2, 3, 4, 5, 6, 7
Five Minutes
Blossom Queen, Barbarian
The Secret
The Family Line
End of the Flies
With Death You Get the Eggroll
The Penguin Sleeps With The Fishes
Only The Worthy
Hero For A Day
End of Empire
Strange Bedfellows
Big Business
A Perfect Crime
The Wise Guy and The Pirates
In Search of the Perfect Cup
T.I.N. Men
The Legend of G and the Dragonettes

The Incredible Mr. Fix-It
Lock Stock and Barrel
Divided Loyalties
Cave of Wonders
A Family Empire
Until We Meet Again
Dragon Rising

Presents Anthology Series
Tales of Urban Fantasy
Five Tales of Bizarre Detectives
Tales of Mystery and Suspense
Tales of Weird Fantasy
Spies, Detectives, & Heroes
Tales of Twisted Crime
Tales of The Unexpected
Tales From Space
10 by Russ Crossley
Round Up At The Burger Bar: The Story of Trixie Pug,
Parts 1- 5 The Beginning
Worlds of Science Fiction and Fantasy
More Tales of Mystery and Suspense
Ladies of the Jolly Roger
Justice Served

Titles as R.G. Hart

Short Stories
Tikka's Big Day
"My Partner the Zombie" —
Hungry For Your Love Anthology
(St. Martin's Press)
Big Hairy Deal
One Red Shoe
A Bad Day in Lunden Texas
Hook Island
Grind Manor

Bloody Betty, Queen of the Pirates

Anthologies
Love Stories

Novels
My Zombie Prince
Antique Virgin
The Fire In Their Hearts
with R.S. Meger (coming soon from Champagne Books)
Zomopolis

Also available from 53rd Street Publishing.

In this thrilling, adventure-laden, grease-stained, booze-soaked comedy spanning the galaxy of tomorrow, two unlikely heroes find each other as they struggle to save addiction for all human and alien kind. Join fast food junkie, Jalapeno Popover, and booze-hound Bud Wiser, as their two cultures clash in a titanic meeting of two intergalactic species so different it's just plain goofy.Attack of the Lushites tells the harrowing story of mail clerk, Jal Popover who, at risk of losing his fat-and-sassy job forever, must deliver the first mail received in six-hundred years. It must be bad news.

Fear strikes at his clogged arteries because Jal LOVES his job. How will he watch vids of old movies all night if he loses his waistline-expanding job? The Lushites are coming! The Lushites are coming! What should we do? Where should we hide? Aw, screw it. Let's have lunch…

The book is available as an ebook or in trade paper-back from your favorite on-line retailer or you can order the paperback at your favorite bookstore.

~~amcontent.com/pod-product-compliance
ce LLC
PA
4130626
00005B/1843